A Family For Christmas

A Mail Order Bride
Christian Holiday Romance

Faith Austen

CHAPTER 1

The train came to a stop. Steam rose over the windows, obscuring the tiny station. The bystanders were enveloped in the cloud. Holly squinted, trying to make out their faces from the train's window.

As she did, the aisle filled with passengers eager to get off the train. Ruddy-faced children were shushed as they pulled on their mother's skirts while men secured the luggage. Everyone seemed to have somebody.

Holly looked away from the window, reminding herself that she finally had somebody, too. Even though she'd never seen her destination or even met the people who waited for her, her life was about to begin on the platform of this railway station.

An attendant tipped up his billed cap before opening the door. The first person he helped off the train was a young woman traveling alone, just like Holly.

The woman wore a short jacket with a lacey blouse that buttoned up the back of her neck. Her hair was swept back and pinned in a swirl at the nape of her neck. A smart new bonnet was secured to her head with a grosgrain ribbon bow.

Holly stood and nervously tucked an unruly tendril behind her ear, feeling a bit underdressed for the occasion. A quick look down upon her apparel confirmed her suspicions. Her skirt was wrinkled from the long ride, and her second-hand shoes unfortunately looked like hand-me-downs. The thin leather was so worn that no amount of polish would ever make them sparkle. Holly knew she shouldn't snub charity, but today she wanted to look special.

Sister Maybelle's warm voice filled her thoughts. *You are special, just as all people are special. God has a plan for you; trust in Him and His judgement.*

Holly brushed her skirt and straightened her back. Sister Maybelle was right. Vanity was far less attractive than a wrinkled skirt and well-loved shoes. She had to embrace her new life with a heart as wide-open as the beautiful and wild country she'd traveled through on her way to Oregon.

Holly got in line. When it was her turn to get off the train, the attendant greeted her with a smile as bright as the one he'd given the stylish young woman.

"Here, let me help you," he said.

Before Holly could respond, he had her luggage in one hand and was helping her down the iron steps with the other. When she was on the wooden platform, she thanked him and took her bag in a trembling fist.

"You look nervous," he noted. "You're not getting married to a man you've never met before, are you?"

Holly almost fell over. "Actually, I…well…"

The attendant laughed and gave her a friendly pat on the shoulder. "Don't worry. Many young women come out West searching for something, and most of them find what they're looking for."

Holly's throat felt tight. She knew it was foolish. The man was merely making chitchat and meant nothing by it. However, she could do nothing to dampen the hope that swelled in her heart.

"Good luck!" he called out before stepping back up the iron steps to help the next passenger off the train.

"Thank you," Holly whispered, though she doubt he heard her. His attention was now entirely focused on the next passenger.

Taking a deep breath, she stepped forward. Turning her head quickly from side to side, she scanned the platform for anyone who might respond to the sight of her.

She'd received no picture of Frank Motherwell, and hadn't sent him one either. He said he didn't care what she looked like, which suited her just fine. Then, he'd said if it mattered to her, he'd arrange to have one taken; however, he preferred saving the money to spend on something more useful. Holly had readily agreed with him, but now that she searched the crowd of strangers after her long journey, she wished she could find a familiar face.

A couple suddenly bolted forward from the crowd. Holly held her breath. She hadn't expected to see a woman accompany the gentleman. What did this mean? Frank Motherwell had said he was a widower. Could this be his sister?

A smile grew across the gentleman's face and the couple picked up their pace, coming directly at her. Though her face grew warm and her hands felt cold as ice.

Now that they were a couple paces away, Holly couldn't help but compare herself to the pretty young woman on the man's arm. Though not unseemly, Holly had never been considered a beauty. Still, she was a hard worker and had a good heart—or at least that was what Sister Maybelle believed. Holly knew many men did not appreciate such hardy qualities, but some did. Frank Motherwell had said he didn't care what she looked like. Was he telling the truth?

Suddenly, the woman by his side spread out her arms in the universal sign of embrace. Holly inadvertently felt a tug at her heart despite her confusion. Then, the woman cried out, "Sarah! We are over here!"

Stumbling, Holly looked over her shoulder and discovered the source of their joy. Another young lady stepped down to the platform and received her luggage from the assistant. Her blonde curls bounced as she returned the couple's smiles brightly. The woman and man rushed around her to embrace her.

She's probably their daughter, Holly thought. *She looks so loved.* Though Holly felt a pang in her heart, her observation contained no envy or malice. Still, she couldn't help but hope that one day she'd be able to embrace another with such candor.

Her throat tightened. She wondered if she should loosen the top two buttons of her blouse, but decided against it. Frank Motherwell wanted someone dependable; she couldn't appear sloppy.

She glanced once more at the reunited family. She was nothing more than a bystander. What had possessed her to make such a long journey away from the only home she'd ever known? Yes, she couldn't stay at the orphanage forever, but Oregon was so far from Massachusetts she might as well have gone to Timbuktu.

Holly took another deep breath in and blew out slowly, reminding herself that she had already left this in God's hands. Life as she known it had been measured out in teaspoons, to make sure that every girl and boy in the orphanage received the same and there was enough for all. This new life she had yet to discover the measure of. She must try not to jump to conclusions.

From the corner of her eye, Holly spied a tall, slender man near the carriages and horses tied at the edge of the station. The man's forehead was furrowed and his eyes cast down to avoid the bright sunlight. He held the hand of a sandy-haired girl who looked to be the age of ten.

Holly felt a pang of sympathy for these two. Despite the father's severe countenance, she could tell he was still a young man. No deep lines creased his face, and he had a full head of thick, dark hair. The little girl's expression cut her even deeper. Instead of joy, indifference seemed wrapped around her tiny shoulders like a shawl. Both of them looked too old and subdued for their ages.

Holly remembered the distant, sorrowful tone in Frank Motherwell's letters. Was this the man she had responded to?

She touched the linen handkerchief in her coat pocket. The words of Sister Maybelle, the five foot bundle of energy and utility who ran the orphanage, filled her mind: *You are off to get married. Put your best foot forward. No need for a new boot if you have a flounce in your long skirt. Here's a handkerchief for luck and comfort.*

Sister Maybelle's simple wisdom soothed her as much as the smooth handkerchief. That memory of love and best wishes gave her a surge of strength. Without wavering, Holly looked into the eyes of the man she knew would be her future husband.

"Holly Warren?" the man inquired softly.

Holly answered his question with another, "Frank Motherwell?"

He nodded abruptly and reached down for her valise and carpet bag with a long leather handle, allowing her to carry her own parasol and private bag.

Her future husband offered no words other than his simple greeting. Holly smiled as she decided to give her attention to the young girl. "Are you Emily?" she asked.

Emily nodded and moved closer to her father.

Holly's smile deepened. She remembered being Emily's age and hiding in Sister Maybelle's skirts. "You are very grown up for a nine-year-old girl."

"I'm nearly ten," Emily frowned and insisted in a flat and slightly sharp voice.

"Of course you are. And where is young Jake?" Holly asked.

Emily pointed towards the station.

A small boy tended to a horse and cart. He pet the horse's long neck even though it was tied, offering comfort in the wake of the loud and busy station. When the boy looked up, Holly's throat tightened.

It was Jake. There could be no confusion, for the young boy was the spitting image of his father, only fashioned on a quarter of the scale. He removed a man's hat that was far too big (but would perfectly fit his father) and wiped his brow. When Jake caught sight of them approaching, he frowned and Holly once again found herself the recipient of the inquisitive look she'd received just moments before.

"This is Holly," Frank told the boy.

Jake nodded once with the intensity of a drill sergeant. "I figured."

Holly bent over, offering her hand. "Hello, Jake."

"Hello." He reached out and gripped her hand firmly, giving it a sturdy shake. Then, he let go and pointed to her personal bag. "I'll take that."

"Thank you." Holly couldn't help but smile at the sincere way he went about his business. He must have gotten his work ethic from his father.

"Come, I'll help you up," Frank told Holly. He gripped the side of the wagon with one hand and held up the other, ready to catch her if she should fall.

"Are you alright?" he asked.

Holly nodded furiously, unwilling to appear flustered in front of her fiancé. *Too late*, she realized as the furrow in Frank's brow deepened.

"I thought you said in your letter that you were prepared for work and accustomed to it."

Holly's mouth dropped open, so shocked at Frank's quick dismissal that for a second she couldn't speak.

"Work at the farm is only going to get harder, especially since it's winter," her previously silent husband continued.

Well! Holly crossed her arms over her chest too, mimicking her husband's gesture. "Everyone works together and takes care of one another at the orphanage. I'm well accustomed to hard work, and more than willing to take on any job that needs to be done. It was how Sister Maybelle raised us. Idle hands are the devil's workshop."

Franks expression softened. "I didn't mean to offend you. I just want you to know that I can't offer much, and the things I can offer must also be earned through dedication and hard work. I won't force you to honor this commitment if this isn't the right life for you."

Holly uncrossed her arms, touched by his sincere concern. "You've already paid for my transport and marriage license."

"And I'd pay for your transport back," Frank responded.

Before Holly had a chance to respond, the cart jostled and creaked. She looked back, startled, to find Jake securing her luggage. She decided to sit so she could better weather the unpredictable movements of the cart. When she returned her attention to Frank, he was focused on attending to Emily.

The little girl tugged on her father's coat until he gently picked her up and set her down next to him in the front of the cart.

Holly couldn't have been more touched by the scene. Frank's love for his children was obvious in his every gesture, and his generosity was evident in his offer for Holly. She knew how much the humble farmer had worked and saved so he could pay for both his advertisement and her ticket. Still, his children needed a mother; obviously, Frank had decided that no sacrifice was too great if it was for his children's sake.

Many had warned Holly against going West. Sure, there were few decent prospects for a poor woman back in Massachusetts, but a woman out here was at the mercy of the wilderness and her future husband. Holly had considered following Sister Maybelle's example and joining a nunnery. All children in the world deserved the love of a father and mother, but some did not get it. Holly, being one of those children, knew this well. Sister Maybelle had filled both roles for many, and proved time and again that the amount of love the human heart was capable of was truly limitless. Still, Sister Maybelle would never have a family of her own.

A few months ago, on her way home from interviews at manors and humble shops, Holly had seen Frank's advertisement in the window of a Mail Order Bride agency. His simple request for a wife in name only to help raise children and tend a home had touched her heart. A few letters later, Holly had hastily licked and pressed down the postage on a letter wherein her whole future was folded and enveloped. One moment she was a spinster; by the time the post returned, she was a mail order fiancé.

Sister Maybelle alone had supported her decision. When Holly asked why, Sister Maybelle told her that her faith in the Lord would be justified. Silently, Holly gave the Lord thanks for delivering her unto a family who had health, strength, and love. These were gifts of inestimable value.

But Holly did not have long to pray. Life in the country moved at a different pace, and she welcomed this change. Soon Frank was helping Jake into the cart. The latter, of course, declared at length that he did not need any help, which prompted Frank to immediately agree even as his son jumped from his knee to the cart.

"See, I can do it myself," Jake told Holly as he took his seat.

"I can see that," Holly replied, looking at her husband in a new light. It was a rare man who could salvage a young boy's pride.

Frank finally got in and took hold of the reins as Emily snuggled up next to him. "We will meet pastor Smith and his second wife, Carol, at the church. Smith will marry us and after that we will return home to the farm."

Home. Holly's heart swelled with warmth despite Frank's bleak delivery of their morning itinerary. For the first time in her life, she'd be able to call a place home.

CHAPTER 2

The quaint white church was situated in a field between a leafless cherry tree orchard and a small forest of pine. Though gray clouds gathered overhead, the sun still shone brightly.

Frank gently pulled on the reigns and the horses stopped. Immediately, Jake jumped from the back of the cart and began tending to them.

"Thank you," Frank called out.

Jake made a noncommittal grunt, but his chest puffed with pride. Frank then set down the reins and got off the cart, trusting Jake's abilities. Holly found that she trusted them, too. Jake obviously knew his way around horses; his father had taught him well.

Frank helped Emily down and then offered Holly his hand. Silently she accepted it, surprised by its warmth. His grip was firm, yet gentle. Holly could tell from his calloused hands that this was a man who embraced his responsibilities and the work that came with caring for them.

"Put your hand on my shoulder," he told her.

Holly did. She leaned on him as she jumped down, and his muscles tensed under her full weight.

Her shoes hit the ground, sloshing in the mud.

"Are you alright?" he asked.

"Yes," she responded.

Frank nodded and looked at the church, expression darkening. "Let's get this over with."

Holly's tight smile froze on her face, and she was glad Frank Motherwell's attention was not on her. Frank had made it clear in his letters that they would be husband and wife in name only. As a widower who'd lost someone he'd cared for deeply, he harbored no romantic notions towards her. He needed a woman to act as a mother to his children and to help out on the farm, nothing more.

Still, his briskness hurt Holly. Yes, their marriage was necessary, but it didn't need to be viewed with the same distaste as dressing a wound.

Frank headed with long strides toward the church. He turned back, "So, are you coming?" He held his hands out, palms up.

"You come too, Emily. Jake can see to Buck on his own."

Emily scowled at Holly, then quickened her pace so she was right behind her father. Holly took a deep breath and started up the small path alone. When she caught up to the two of them, they all went into the dark church together.

"Thanks for your accommodation, pastor Smith," Frank called out.

A man with snowy hair got up from the pew and stood. He looked like he'd once been a tall man. Now, he was stooped over and frail, though his smile was even brighter than the rose and golden light streaming from the stained glass window.

"Frank!" he said, "good to see you!"

Frank gave a noncommittal grunt, but the pastor didn't mind. Instead, he turned to Holly and gave her a firm shake. "Holly Warren, I presume? I'm Pastor James Smith. Welcome to Sweet Western's humble church."

"And don't forget his wife, Carol!" a cheerful, feminine voice from behind the altar called. An older woman emerged, carrying a vase full of flowering sagebrush, juniper, baby's breath, and holly. "When I heard you'd be coming off the train, I scrambled to get some flowers together to commemorate your arrival."

She then handed the flowers to the momentarily speechless Holly.

"Thank you," Holly was finally able to reply. She could barely believe the hospitality and joy that was radiating from the happy couple.

Carol placed a hand over her heart. She was an ample woman, like Holly imagined Jack Spratt's wife to be. "Oh, you poor dear. Imagine being a mail order bride and coming so far and then getting married the same day you arrive!"

Holly blushed at Carol's reference to being married as soon as she arrived. She and her husband were little more than strangers, and she couldn't begin to imagine what the happy couple thought of her arrangement.

"We don't want to impose on you," Frank said abruptly. "So we'd like to do the ceremony now, if that's alright."

"Of course," Carol smiled. She then went over to the organ, sat, and started playing the refrain to the Wedding March.

Frank interrupted her song, "We don't need the trimmings. I just wanted us to be wed."

Carol immediately stopped playing. Holly's eyes went wide. She didn't quite know what to think. How could Frank act so rude to the hospitable pastor and his wife? In a church? In front of his child? She glanced at poor Emily.

The girl seemed to stand in one place and shuffle at the same time. Her head was downturned, and her hair hung over her face like barriers. Holly couldn't make out the expression on her face. Oh, this was not how a little girl should be on the day her father was to be married!

Holly's worries turned inward. Was her new husband unhappy with her? Did he expect a different kind of woman to step off the train? Holly tried to sense what Frank was feeling, but even though he was close, he seemed more distant than his daughter Emily.

Maybe Holly should have listened to all the naysayers back in Massachusetts. What did she really know about Frank? He was just a man who had sent fare for her ticket. They'd made a bargain, and now they were sealing that bargain with a wedding ceremony. There'd been no talk of romance, only marriage. But still, Holly had hoped he would be open to friendship. She gripped the bouquet, praying for guidance on how she should proceed.

Pastor Smith stepped forward, still smiling. "Of course, Frank. As such an upstanding and helpful member of our community, it is my honor to marry you." He then winked at Holly.

Holly gulped. She had a feeling that Pastor Smith's reassuring words were for her benefit, which suggested he believed this match could work. Holly thought back on what she'd discovered about Frank in the short time she'd been with him. He loved his children. He cared for his animals. He was dependable. Holly felt in her heart that this was a man she could count on. As the small ceremony continued, Holly's resolve grew stronger. This was a man she wanted to stand aside and help.

Pastor Smith turned to Holly. "Do you take this man to be your lawfully wedded husband?"

Holly looked at Frank Motherwell, this time studying him as a woman. With a long nose, high cheekbones, and distinct brows, his visage as not quite handsome. If they were at a country ball, he wouldn't be the first man a young lady would notice. Still, she'd feel a flutter of butterflies in her stomach if he were the one who asked her to dance.

There was something alluring about his rugged features. Sturdy as mountains, wild as the wind blowing through the plains. Despite his stoic demeanor, his eyes were as expressive and expansive as an Oregon sky.

At that moment, it was his eyes that captivated Holly. He seemed to look at her without quite looking at her. And though he tried hard to hide it, Holly felt his sadness as keenly as if it were rain seeping through her clothes.

Did Pastor Smith marry Frank and his previous wife Margaret in this very church? Is that why he felt so distant from her now?

Holly did not seek to replace his wife. She wished she could communicate that to him plainly right now, but she knew such words would go unheard. Even if his heart were open enough to hear it, Holly knew he wouldn't appreciate an audience.

However, there was something she could say in front of an audience. Such words would probably hurt to hear and also go unappreciated, but she needed to say them to him.

She took a step forward, looking deeply into his wounded eyes. "I, Holly Warren, take you, Frank Motherwell, to be my lawfully wedded husband. To have and to hold, from this day forward. For better, for worse. For richer and for poorer. In sickness and in health, until death do us part."

Frank's Adam's apple bobbed.

Pastor Smith turned to him. "Do you take this woman to be your lawfully wedded wife?"

Frank shut his eyes. "I do," he whispered. "I do."

Her heart swelled. Maybe it wasn't much as far as vows went, but she knew how much strength it took him to say those words—to admit to himself, even for a moment, that he needed a partner. That is what they were now: partners. One day, they would also be friends.

Looking down, Frank took Holly's hand in his. She was surprised by the callouses on his fingers, and by the warmth of his touch despite the cold. The small gold band he slipped onto her finger like silk. When she looked down, she was happy to find the ring fit her finger quite well.

CHAPTER 3

After the ceremony, they bundled into the wagon once more. Holly sat down with a thump upon the wagon's rough wood seat. Emily slid in effortlessly between her and Frank and snuggled next to her father's thin legs. Jake once again slipped into the back to guard Holly's luggage.

Frank clicked his tongue and the horse strode away from the church. Everyone was quiet on the ride back to the Motherwell's farm, giving Holly the impression that they were heading off to a funeral instead of returning home. Even the landscape seemed to mourn. Black birds cawed, there were traces of frost on the puddles, crisp sound of hoofbeat upon the road bare of dirt and pounded hard to a rock base. Holly briefly wondered if the land itself was as barren as these individuals who lived and gained a living upon it.

The carriage gave a bump once in awhile. Holly slid up against Emily and then placed her hand on the rail near the bench and pulled herself back as she noticed the child stiffen and shrug further against her father. Holly turned to look back at Jake but could only see the back of his hat as he watched the wheels spinning and the road retreating past an isolated farmhouse or shed or cow.

The cart bundled once more but this time Holly straightened her back, unwilling to give into another bout of self-pity. God had set her on this path for good reason. She gave a silent prayer to God to ease this family's suffering. She also asked him for the strength to do what was right. When she opened her eyes once more, Holly took in her surroundings with a sense of pride instead of wallowing in despair.

The grass along the road was yellowed, dark thistles stood alongside ratty cattails. Holly wondered if there was any wild game here. She silently thanked Sister Maybelle again for her lessons in the kitchen.

She could provide all the things a mother could give these young children. All but their mother's love. Perhaps her own love would suffice.

She looked up and saw a line of trees bordering a field on the hillside. Most of the leaves were laid to rest at the foot of those trees, but a few clung stubbornly to the branches. They were vibrant red and brilliant gold, and when the wind made them turn, it gave them the appearance of a gentle flame in the hearth.

Speaking of a hearth, Holly saw a wisp of smoke trailing upwards.

The horse's ears pricked forward. He raised his nose and his gait incrementally speeded though Frank held the reins as steadily as before. Without a word from this stony family, Holly knew that she had already spied their home.

Without a tug on the reins the horse turned down the narrow lane. The carriage jostled her even though she held on fast. This time the bumps were enough to unseat Emily, who was lifted up so high that she nearly landed on Holly's lap. The girl quickly shuffled back into her seat and Holly laid a quiet hand upon her shoulder for a short moment.

Holly raised her chin and surveyed her first home.

Another horse stood in the distance, watching them. Beside the mare was a medium sized barn with a few holes on the sides. The roof looked worn but patched. Frank pulled the wagon up to the barn. Holly smelled the rich scent of hay and then a sour stench, of pigs perhaps. It was strongly astringent with a hint of spoiled sweetness.

The rustic house had a covered porch along the broadside. Wide wooden steps lead up to the porch. Faded curtains hung like lank hair on either side of the windows. This home was sorely in need of cheer and a woman's touch. She wondered if she would be enough. Perhaps she could turn their lives around and the farm could thrive again. That would be a suitable goal: just get everyone back on their feet again.

Holly stole a glance at Frank—*no, at her husband*, she corrected. She sensed no relief coming from him even though they'd reached their destination. His unreadable eyes faced forward. They reminded of her ground water that didn't abide being stirred, as though their preferred state was to be as still as glass without any reflection.

Frank's gaze remained steady and forward until he pulled the horse to a stop. He got out of the carriage, his long leg making the step to the ground without any change in the level of his head. Dutifully, he came around to her side of the carriage and helped his new wife off the carriage. He then offered his hand to his daughter.

"No," Emily said. "*I* can do it."

"Are you certain?" Frank asked. "The ground is slippery."

"Of course," Emily said, beaming at Holly. "*I'm* a *big girl*." Then, the young girl eschewed her father's help and jumped lightly down from the carriage, with an exaggerated ease.

Frank shook his head as Jake silently saw to Holly's luggage. "Well," he said, planting his hand down on his daughter's shoulder, "big girls can help others inside, can't they? Why don't you show you're new—um, Holly around while Jake and I take care of the carriage."

Emily's mouth dropped open. "Why do I have to do that?"

Frank stepped back, sighing. "Emily…"

"I don't want to! She's not my mother!"

The sound of little Emily's voice seemed to echo through the open air. Every muscle in Holly's body tensed.

"No one said she was your mother," Frank continued quietly. "But she's going to be staying with us."

"*And* making your food," Jake added, narrowing his eyes at Holly. "You better be nice to her, or else she'll poison you."

Emily gasped, clutching her threadbare coat.

"Jake!" Frank interjected sharply. "Don't lie to your sister. No one is poisoning anybody."

"How do you know, dad?" Jake asked. "You just sent her a letter. Mom said no one can read your handwriting. This lady probably didn't even read it before she came out here!"

"Jake, go tend to the horses," Frank directed. "And think about what you just said."

"Oh, I'll think about it alright," Jake muttered as he led the horse to the barn.

However, the damage had already been done. Poor Emily was worked up. "You didn't read it!" she told Holly. "And if she did, that's even worse!"

Frank scowled, returning his attention to his daughter. "Calm down, Emily. Why would that be worse?"

Emily's fists shook at her sides. "Because if she did, then she why would she want to come here? Why would she want to be with us?"

Emily's eyes glistened with unshed tears. Holly's heart broke. She wanted more than anything to gather the girl in her arms and hug her, but she knew an embrace would be unwelcome. Instead, she tried to sooth Emily's pain with her words.

"It is true that your father's handwriting was difficult to read, but I managed after some effort," Holly said, bending over so that her eyes were on the same level as Emily's. "You may not believe this, but much of why I wanted to come out here had to do with you and Jake."

"You wanted to punish us?" Emily asked with a shaking voice.

"No. I wanted to help you," Holly insisted. "You see, I grew up in an orphanage all alone, and every night before I went to sleep, I prayed for a family—"

"Well you can't steal ours!" Emily yelled. Tears now streamed freely down her rosy cheeks, and her bright eyes blazed with sorrow.

Holly's chest tightened. Had she just made things worse? *Oh Lord*, she prayed, *please help me find the words to make this right.*

Frank stepped in. "Emily, that's enough."

But Emily was beyond listening to anyone, even her father's warning. Instead of stopping, she screamed, "You can't steal my mother just because your mother didn't want you!"

"Emily! I said that's enough!"

Frank didn't yell at his daughter, but his voice had a hardness to it that made Holly shiver. Emily looked up at her father in shock. Her bottom lip trembled.

Frank put his hand over his mouth. "Emily," he whispered.

Emily stumbled back.

"Emily, I'm sorry," he said, reaching out to her. "I didn't mean to—"

Emily didn't let him finish. Instead, she turned and ran to the house, her little feet slipping but she refused to fall. With every misstep she moved faster until she was barreling through the front door of the humble farmhouse.

Frank took a few steps after her before he too slipped. But unlike his daughter, after he regained his footing, he stopped, defeated.

"I'm sorry for her outburst," he said without turning. "She should not have spoken to you that way."

"It is alright. She's in pain," Holly soothed.

"No it isn't," he said. "I should not have spoken to her that way."

Holly couldn't help but notice the tension in his shoulders. She wanted to softly rub his back the way Sister Maybelle had whenever someone needed comfort, but knew instinctively that her touch would be even less welcome to Frank as it would have been to Emily.

Instead, she stood beside her new husband and said without looking, "Emily will forgive you. She loves you, and knows that you love her."

Frank looked at his hands. "I have never raised my voice to a child," he whispered.

Holly smiled at her husband's hands. They were so large and strong. Yet, at the same time, they were gentle...and perhaps even more than that, they were willing to reach out for help when they needed it. Yes, his voice had been stern, but it hadn't been cruel; that also showed her what kind of man he was. "We all do and say things we wish we could take back. A few harshly spoken words will not create an irreversible rift between father and daughter, especially when there is so much love between you. Talk to her."

He gulped. "We haven't done much talking much, lately."

Holly nodded. She figured as much. Both children on the ride home had been too comfortable with silence. There was value in contemplation; as it was written in Isaiah: *Repentance and rest was one's salvation, and quietness and trust was one's strength.* But Frank had proven his strength; what he needed now was faith. And even more than that, his children needed their father. Holly knew that the end to this family's grief relied on them coming together, not remaining in solitude.

"If you haven't talked to her much lately, then you must start," Holly told him. "Emily wants your guidance. If you direct your children onto the right path, then when they are older, they will not leave it."

Frank looked up at her as she said her last words. His blue eyes studied her so deeply that she shivered.

"That is a beautiful thought, Holly. Did you come up with that?" he asked.

"No," Holly replied quickly. "It is from Proverbs."

"Proverbs?" Frank repeated, scowling. "The Bible?"

Suddenly, Frank looked very much like he had back in church. Holly wasn't sure what the source of her husband's scorn was, but she knew there was no shame in sharing God's word. "Yes," she said, keeping her back straight.

Frank turned away from her, but not before she saw a flash of pain cross his expression. "I'll talk to

Emily. But Holly, in the future, I'd prefer it if you did not offer any wisdom from that book."

Holly's mouth was agape. Even though she stood still, she felt as if she'd lost her footing. "What do you mean?"

"It is not your fault. I should have been clear in my letter," Frank began, stuffing his hands into the pockets of his coat and turning his back to Holly once more. "I will not ask you to abandon your faith; if you are capable of finding comfort in it, then cling to that comfort as long as you can. There are many good Christians in this town, and I count many as close friends."

Holly's heart was beating so fast she almost couldn't make out his words. What was her husband saying?

Frank looked to the barn he watched Jake take the horse inside, giving Holly a good look at his devastated profile. "All I ask is that you keep your love of God to yourself."

"What do you mean I must keep it to myself? Can I pray?"

Frank's shoulders relaxed. "Of course. You can do anything you would do normally. Just don't involve us."

"Can I pray for you, then?" Holly asked. "Because that's what I would do normally. I would pray for all of us, including Emily and Jake."

Frank's jaw tightened. "Fine, if that's what you want. Just don't do it out loud. I don't want to listen to it." He turned back to the house, and before walking back to the house, finished by saying: "I know you may not understand, but there will be no God for me or for my children."

CHAPTER 4

Holly wrapped her arms around her chest. Frank's words echoed in her mind, leaving her feeling as hollow and cold as he had looked before he left.

There will be no God for me or for my children.

She shut her eyes. It wasn't her place to judge. As Sister Maybelle had told the children at the orphanage numerous times, all people have their own path in life. Holly truly believed all good men and women would be saved. Frank was also a good man…which was why his sorrow touched her so deeply.

Holly believed with all her heart that Frank deserved happiness and to live in the warmth of God's grace. Still, she wouldn't force him. He had to come to the understanding that he was worthy of God's love on his own.

She opened her eyes, taking in the small house and her grandiose surroundings. All around her, from the snow-capped mountains to the old growth trees framing the quaint farm, Holly saw evidence of God's love. If only Frank could see it; if only he could see that he was loved.

She clasped her hands before her lips. Frank had told her to keep her love of God to herself, and she had every intention of following his order. Still, that wouldn't stop her from praying for him.

Sister Maybelle believed that those who did not pray for themselves needed to be prayed for the most. There were so many lost souls in Massachusetts that had strayed from the right path and needed salvation. However, there was another category of people who needed God's love just as much.

Sorrow tainted everything, especially joy. It was hard to see God's beauty while grieving. Happiness became a betrayal instead of something to celebrate.

Holly always prayed sincerely for everyone, but the prayers she offered for those who doubted whether they were worthy of God's love were especially close to her heart because she knew what it was like to feel abandoned.

Though she never met Margaret, Holly knew that she had been a good person. The children she brought into this world were full of so much promise and strength. That was why they felt the loss of their mother so keenly, and why they were able to be there to help their father. Frank had obviously dedicated his life to his wife, otherwise Frank would not still grieve so deeply. The marriage they enjoyed had been built on a foundation of love and hard work. Margaret had been a partner and a friend in addition to a wife.

Which was why Holly knew that Margaret would not want her husband to continue to suffer.

Holly bowed her head and quieted her mind and began to pray.

Lord, thank you for delivering me to Frank Motherwell and his beautiful children. Margaret, thank you for sharing this life with me. I know that if you were still alive, we would be friends, and I will cherish the gift of your family.

Please, walk with me, give me the strength to raise Emily and Jake the way you would want them to be raised. If I must discipline them, please let me do so with a gentle hand so it never feels like punishment, so they never doubt even for one moment that they are loved and worthy of love.

And please let me be a good partner for Frank. I do not need a sensational romance, I only wish to be his friend. Help me to become the kind of woman he can depend on for help, to trust with his sorrows, and to help him once again learn to love himself. I know everyone's path is their own and I do not doubt your judgement, Lord; I will not preach or try to usurp his position. I only ask that he knows your love and Grace even if he cannot yet accept it in name, for he is a good man and does not deserve a life of suffering. Please, help me show him that allowing joy to reenter his heart is not a betrayal of his love for his wife, but an expression of it, for I know that Margaret, also, would not want to see him in pain.

Holly lowered her hands. A beam of sunlight streamed from the cloudy sky, and her heart felt at peace. She walked into the house, filled with new purpose.

The inside of the house was simple—some mismatched chairs, a table that looked like it had been in the family for a long time, and rugs that had been

made by tying together scraps of torn shirts and rags.
Holly supposed some back in Massachusetts might
have dismissed such a place as rustic, but to her it felt
cozy. Life out here might sometimes be hard, but
people worked together and found joy in each other's
company. The greatest joy came from family. That
was the kind of joy she came to Oregon to find, and
the kind of joy she hoped to reintroduce to the
Motherwells.

Still, there was work to be done. Holly shivered as
the door closed behind her. *The fire in the wood stove
must be low,* she thought. She opened the door and
threw in a small log about the scale of a limb of a tree.
The hungry maw of the stove flared a moment and
then she shut the door tight with a latch. With that
done, she decided to take in her surroundings.

Holly stood and looked around the room. The
main room was ample in size but still cozy. In her
mind she removed the clutter and debris and saw it
whole and put into order. It would be more than
suitable. She walked slowly with deliberate steps into
the kitchen. There she sighed. There were heaps of
dishes in the sink. More still on the counter. There
was a solid slab of wood that served as a cutting
board but it was covered in grease, as though a pig

Faith Austen

had been butchered on it. The floor could be seen in patches. It seemed to serve mostly as the last place for smaller things to land. Like the house was a threshing place, where chaff was pulled from the wheat and the bran fell to the bottom. Holly was suddenly seized by a flurry of energy.

Near the wood stove was a cushioned seat that had a basket of mending beside it. Holly admired the needlepoint flowers on the cushion. Despite being the most comfortable chair in the room, the cushion was dusty. It must have been where Margaret's sat.

Beside the chair was a basket of mending. There was a cotton sheet in there, too threadbare for much use other than for patching behind a tear. There were also a few items of clothing that were barely held together with buttons sewn in strange places and uneven stitches. Holly's heart swelled with pride as she took inventory of these items. They were unmistakably done by Emily, who had bravely decided to take on her mother's work after her death. Once again, Holly admired the small girl's strength. Though she needed practice, her mother had obviously taught her well and endowed her with a Christian work ethic. She knew Margaret would also be proud.

Holly heard a small cough. She turned to find Emily staring at her toes with her father right behind her.

Holly couldn't help but smile, even though she knew Emily couldn't see it. Carefully, she set down the small girl's work.

Frank's face, however, remained tired. "Emily has something to say to you."

"I can say it myself, father," Emily whispered.

"Alright," Frank said, patting his daughter on the shoulder. Then, he looked up at Holly. "I'll be in the barn helping Jake if either of you need me."

Emily said nothing.

Frank squeezed her shoulder. "You can do it," he whispered near his daughter.

"I know I can," Emily replied.

"That's right. You're a big girl, now. Big enough to show Holly how to take care of the house." Frank gave her another pat and then pulled a long gray scarf off the hook near the door. Even from her vantage point in the room, Holly could see it had been eaten by moths.

"Now," Frank said, "I've got to go make sure Jake hasn't tied up the chickens and led the horse to the chicken coup."

Emily giggled despite herself. Frank gave her a tender, aching smile as he wrapped the scarf around his neck. His expression sobered just before he left. "Tell her, Emily."

Emily sighed. "I will."

"Good. See you soon." And with that, he was out the door.

Pouting, Emily turned her attention to Holly. "My father wants me to tell you I'm sorry for saying those mean things to you."

"Apology accepted," Holly said. "Now, is there a broom in the house?" She couldn't wait to start cleaning; she had a lot to do and not much light left in the day.

Emily frowned. "Aren't you going to ask me if I'm really sorry, or if I'm just saying it because father told me to?"

"No," Holly said.

Emily's frown deepened. "Why not?"

Holly cocked her head to the side, unsure of how to proceed. *Lord, please let me find the right words to say*, she prayed. "My guess is that you don't think you're sorry, and that you're upset your father made you apologize in the first place. That's alright; I know you're angry that I'm here, and I know that you wish I would go away. That's what you're feeling right now, at least. However, your true feelings go deeper than that."

Emily now frowned with confusion. "I don't understand."

"You *are* sorry, Emily, even though you don't know it," Holly said softly. "You're sorry because it isn't in your nature to hurt someone else, and when you realize this you will feel guilty. At that time, I want you to remember that I have already forgiven you so that you can forgive yourself."

The frown and the confusion on Emily's face had disappeared. "What if I'm not actually sorry?" she asked in a voice filled with uncertainty. "What if I'm a bad girl?"

"You're not a bad girl. Don't ever think that," Holly told her. "And don't worry about what you're feeling right now. A stranger has come to live in your home, and that must be scary."

"I'm not scared of you!" Emily insisted.

Holly grinned. "Good, because right now I need a lot of help. Do you you know where a broom is?"

Emily nodded.

"Will you get it for me?" Holly prompted.

Emily nodded again and scurried out of the room. A moment later, Holly heard the sound of rusty hinges and of wood being dragged over the floor. The light footsteps became distant and low. Then, there was a loud thud as the wood came down again and the footsteps returned, growing louder.

Emily held the staff of the broom high above her head so the broom corn wouldn't touch the floor. The broom was lovely. It had a delicate handle, sized for a woman's hand. It was bound in a flare and also sensibly covered with a strip of leather. The broom corn was springy and ample and long.

After taking this in, Holly gave Emily a smile that could barely contain her surprise and joy. "Thank you, Emily!" she said. "This is exactly what I needed!"

Emily's grip on the broom tightened. She seemed loath to let it go, but finally said, "It was mother's. Take good care of it."

Holly's heart grew warm as she realized just how much of a gift she was receiving from the little girl. "I will," she assured little Emily. "Where was it?"

"The cellar," Emily told her, handing the broom over.

Holly gripped the marvelous broom in her hand and knew she could set this house right. "Emily, I am going to start cleaning. Will you get a large kettle of hot water boiling?"

Emily nodded and, once again, took off. Holly smiled, touched by Emily's sincerity.

Though the little girl's feelings about the new woman her father had married were undoubtedly mixed, she was eager to help and took her work seriously.

However, Holly had little time for her musings. There was work to be done.

Unfortunately, she had little time for sweeping. She'd have to do as much as she could as quickly as possible and then finish later. Plumes of dust spilled out in front of her. The cleared-off floor boardss beneath her feet seemed to glow as if they were as pleased as her to be rid of the dust. Holly knew that with another round of sweeping and a mop she'd be able to make them sparkle, but that would have to come later. Frank and Jake would soon be returning from their work in the barn hungry, and little Emily's stomach would undoubtedly be growling from all of her help. There was nothing as satisfying as a warm supper after a long day, and Holly was determined to treat everybody.

Holly entered the kitchen with excitement. With pride, she hung the broom from a nail beside the door and then went looking for food.

Emily led her to a pantry that was stocked with onions, carrots, leeks, radishes, potatoes, sweet potatoes, asparagus, and other sturdy vegetables. There were sacks full of flour; one a jar of salt, one of sugar, and one of honey; a generous amount of eggs lined up carefully in boxes; and some tart apples. On the top shelf were some canned peaches and cherries. There were also a few biscuits beside them in a basket. Holly noted that the handwriting on these canned items was not Frank's, and wondered if the jam and biscuits were given to him by a kind neighbor.

"Dad said we can get an elk steak from the icebox," she said from the door.

"Elk?" Holly asked.

"Yes. My dad and my uncle hunted one a few months ago."

Holly gulped. She had no idea how to cook an elk. Was it cooked like beef? Yes, it must be. She could deal with that.

"That sounds wonderful, Emily," Holly said. Then, she scowled at the shelves. There wasn't enough time to make a stew, but she could boil some carrots and braise them with honey. The sweetness of cooked onions might subdue the spiciness of radishes. Some asparagus would be good, too. She'd cook them with the steak, sprinkle on some salt, and then serve them together. Holly was unsure of what such a meal might be called, but was certain it would fill the belly.

She turned to Emily. "Have you ever sliced an onion or peeled carrots?"

Emily nodded. "Mother taught me, and I've been doing it all alone for all this time."

Holly hoped the smile she gave the small girl wasn't tinged with sadness, for there was some in her heart. Emily had been so brave in her mother's absence. She had no doubt that the house would have been in far worse shape if she weren't here to take on her mother's tasks. Emily had done so well, and Holly felt honored to continue her education.

"Well, let's cut them together after we've gotten the meat," she said.

Emily nodded, already focused on doing her next job to the best of her abilities.

Holly was determined to do her best, too. With both of them working together, dinner would go perfectly.

Right?

CHAPTER 5

Dinner cooked up nicely. Emily was very helpful. Holly had given her the job of peeling so that Holly, as the adult, could focus on the chopping. After they were done and everything was cooking up in the pot, Emily stirred the vegetables with a militaristic precision. Holly couldn't help but smile as she noted how seriously the young girl took her task. She had no doubt none of the vegetables would be burnt, and the meat would be juicy. Maybe Holly could learn a few things from her new ward.

However, she couldn't sit back and admire Emily for long. There was still one last task to finish. "Keep up the good work, Emily. I'm going to clean the dishes. Then, we can set the table."

Emily nodded without taking her eyes off the pot.

Holly then focused on the stoneware.

She gasped. *Oh dear*, she thought. Many of the dishes and mugs were in very poor condition. She should have noticed this upon her first inspection, but she'd been too excited about cleaning the floor. She wouldn't make that mistake again.

Well, I must focus. There's no turning back the clock, Holly thought. She then started sorting the chipped dishes from the few that were fully intact, and placing those that were broken in box on the floor.

Among the irreparable pieces was a mug with a crack from rim to base. It was handsomely painted, with lean brown branches and delicately rendered cardinals on a snowy white background, but useless. As she added it to the growing pile, Holly heard the front door slam and the soft yet determined thump of a child's footsteps.

"What are you doing?" Jake asked, bending over her pile of hopeless objects.

"Making dinner," Emily said without looking away from the pot.

"And cleaning up a bit," Holly told Jake. "You should get out of your wet clothes and ready for supper."

Jake didn't move. Something in the pile of broken dishes had caught his attention. "What is this doing here?" he asked, rescuing the mug Holly had briefly admired.

"It's broken, Jake," Holly said. As the words left her mouth, she realized she'd made a grave error.

Jake's cheeks became as red as the cardinals on the mug. "This was mother's!" he said, bringing the mug to his chest.

"I'm sorry," Holly said soothingly. "I didn't know."

"You don't know anything!" Jake said.

Holly was surprised by his outburst. Even Emily dropped the wooden spoon she stirred with. It clattered on the floor.

Both children were staring at her. Holly suddenly felt very small. Though these children were young, their grief was strong. As a guardian, she now had the power to govern their development. For some reason, she hadn't thought about this aspect of raising a child on her journey West; instead, she'd only thought of the happiness she'd longed to be a part of.

But being a part of a family wasn't always easy. There would be many trials ahead, and Holly must prove to them and their father that she was up for the task. Hard lessons sometimes had to be learned, and Holly needed to be empathetic *and* fair.

Once again, Holly prayed to God to help her find the right words so she could excel in her new position.

"I'm sorry, Jake," she said, kneeling down so she was lower than the red-cheeked boy. "There are many things I don't know yet. I am eager to learn these things. Many days, I know I will rely on you and Emily for help. However, when someone makes a mistake, you mustn't chastise them for it. Instead, you should help them see the error of their ways so they do not make the same mistake twice. If you make someone feel bad, they'll only remember feeling bad; if you teach someone how to do something right, they'll remember it for the rest of their life."

Jake frowned, clasping the mug to his chest. Holly smiled. "From the moment I saw it, I thought it was a handsome mug, Jake. And while it is cracked, I was wrong for thinking it was no longer useful. Don't you think it would look pretty on the windowsill?"

Jake looked at the mug, and then up at the windowsill. "Yes. The branches on the mug look like the ones on the apple tree."

"You're right." Holly smiled. The boy was very observant. "Do you want to put it up?"

Jake nodded. "Yes. I'll do it," he said, standing up on his tiptoes so he could reach above the cutting board.

Holly did not offer to help him up. Though it was awkward, she knew the boy could do it on his own. More than that, she knew it was important for him to do it on his own; the mug in the window would serve as a reminder that Holly had no intention of taking his mother's place, and in fact respected all that she'd accomplished.

"It looks very nice there," Holly said once he was back on his feet and the mug was securely tucked in the corner of the windowsill. Jake was right, the branches on the mug did resemble the branches of the apple tree outside. Holly knew she would appreciate the view of when a bird rested on the apple tree's branches.

"Thank you," Holly said, turning to Jake. She was surprised to find Jake studying her.

"I'm sorry I said you didn't know anything. There are some things you know," he said.

Holly was happy to see that his eyes looked directly into hers and his voice didn't waver. Like his father, Jake was able to admit when he was wrong and longed to set things right.

"Apology accepted," Holly said.

He took a deep breath. "I guess there are even some things I might learn from you," he added a bit grudgingly.

Holly's smile deepened. "I'm sure we'll both learn many things from each other," she corrected. "Now go change your clothes and wash your hands. Your father will be home soon, and when he arrives he'll want dinner."

Jake's back straightened. "I won't hold anyone up!" he promised, then dashed from the room.

Holly also didn't want to hold anyone up. With Jake and Emily both doing their best with the tasks she gave him, it was up to her to make sure the rest of dinner went smoothly.

She cleaned the rest of the dishes. Some were chipped, but they'd have to do. Jake finished dressing and insisted he help her set the table. Holly was thankful for the help. The two of them got everything ready while Emily kept watch over the food.

As the last fork was set on the table, the front door flew open.

A gust of cold wind toyed with the hem of Holly's skirt as she glanced up.

Frank's strong silhouette stood in the doorframe. Though he must have been tired from hurrying to finish his daily tasks in a quarter of the amount of time he normally spent on them (thanks to the wedding ceremony in town), his back was straight.

Frank stepped forward, shutting the door quietly behind him, careful not to let in another chilly gust.

"Hello father," Jake said, grinning. "I set the table."

Frank turned, raising his eyebrows. "Really?"

"Yes," Jake said, beaming with pride.

Frank shook his head. "That is a first. And look, the forks and knives are all in the right order."

Jake spared me a quick glance. "Holly might have done some of it, but I washed up so I could help!"

Frank patted his son on the head. As he did, he looked at Holly with an expression she couldn't quite make out. Still, it didn't matter. The strange expression was gone almost as soon as it had appeared, for Frank's attention had returned to his son.

"You certainly did wash up," Frank said. "I reckon it will make dinner more pleasant."

Jake pulled away. "Are you saying I stink?"

"Frank's lip quirked up. He glanced at Holly again, this time his eyes dancing with light and humor. "Did I say any such thing?"

Holly couldn't believe it. Had Frank just made a joke?

The importance of this was completely lost on young Jake. "You think I stink!" the boy accused.

"That's because you do!" screamed Emily from the kitchen. "You smell like rotten eggs!"

Frank shook his head. "It's not that bad," he reassured Jake. "Emily, where did you develop such sass?"

"It's not sass, father. It's the truth!" the little girl proclaimed.

Jake tugged on Frank's sleeve. "Do I really smell like rotten eggs?"

"No," Holly reassured. "You smell like a little boy who has been working hard outside, and there is nothing rotten about that."

"And even if you did, you don't anymore. You cleaned up for dinner. You haven't done that since…" Franks' expression became somber. He straightened his back. "Now, what's keeping your sister?"

Jake took his seat at the table, frowning.

"Father!" Emily yelled from the kitchen. "I'm making dinner!"

"Emily has been cooking," Holly explained.

Frank shut his eyes, inhaling deeply. A sliver of a smile once again returned to is lips. "It smells wonderful."

"It better! Holly and I worked hard on it," the little girl called out. A few seconds later she appeared in the doorway. Her mitt was as big as her head, and the apron she wore hit the floor even though Holly had rolled it up. That was alright; she knew she'd grow into her mother's apron soon. Children grew up so fast.

Frank seemed to be contemplating this same sentiment. "You did a great job, Emily."

Emily scrunched up her nose. "How can you tell? You haven't even tasted it."

"But I can smell it, and it smells just like something your mother would make. I think she'd be proud of you."

Emily's grin stretched from ear to ear.

Jake, however, was ready to eat. "Let's get on with it! I'm starving," he said.

Frank frowned at his son. "Jake, be patient."

Jake pouted, but didn't complain again. Instead, he got up and pulled out the chair next to his for his sister. "Come on, Emily."

Emily jumped into the chair, still beaming. Frank lumbered into his own seat.

Holly immediately dashed to the kitchen. Now it was her turn to present the dinner she and Emily had made for their family. The elk steaks smelled lovely and the carrots and onions were cooked to perfection. She grabbed two pot holders and picked up the cast iron pan. Carefully, she picked it up and slowly walked into the room. She wanted to showcase Emily's hard work; the girl deserved to take some pride in it.

When Holly entered, she saw Jake moving a chair from the corner to the table; now the table seated four.

Holly couldn't have been more touched. She thanked Jake simply, and he grunted in return. Though he'd completed this simple task without any sentimentality, Holly knew what it meant. She was beginning to be accepted into their family and she couldn't have been happier.

Holly brought over the pan and passed out the elk steaks. She also set the butter and the biscuits in the center of the table. Everyone sat for a moment. Frank looked it all over with an assessing eye and then reached to butter his biscuits. Jake quickly follow suit and soon his plate was filled. Emily affected nonchalance but Holly could hear her stomach rumble.

Holly left her plate empty. What could she do? She was taught never to eat without having first said Grace. Well, that was fine; she'd honor Frank's wish by saying Grace quietly to herself.

Holly shut her eyes, trying not to be aware of the knife cutting elk meat or buttering bread. She tried not to notice the chewing.

Please dear Lord, forgive my silent thanks. Please understand that I have to obey my husband in this matter. It does not prevent me from thanking your for this food, for the blessing of having my first meal with my new family. For delivering me safely to the Motherwell household. In this and in everything, I am grateful for your blessing and good will. All things come from Thee.

"Why isn't Holly eating?" asked Jake.

"It can't be because the food isn't good," said Frank. "This is delicious, Emily."

"Holly helped me make it," Emily was sure to add. "Holly, why aren't you eating with us?"

Holly opened her eyes and found three sets of eyes on hers. She lifted her napkin and placed it on her lap before answering. "I have been taught never to eat without first giving thanks."

Frank's jaw tightened. He quickly wiped his mouth with his cloth napkin, then set it back down in his lap.

"Thanks to who?" Emily asked.

Holly's fingers fidgeted with her dress. Was it alright to tell them? She had promised Frank she wouldn't make a spectacle of her faith. Still, he had said he would not try to change her faith. However, he couldn't have foreseen this situation. Would he be angry?

"I'm sorry, Emily. I can't say," Holly stammered.

"Why not?" Jake asked.

"Yeah, why can't you say?" Emily added.

Both children were looking at Holly expectantly, but she couldn't bring herself to answer. *Oh Lord,* she prayed, *what is the right thing to do in this situation?*

Frank coughed. "It's fine, Holly. You can tell them. I suppose it's unavoidable."

Holly's eyes darted to him. "But you said…"

"It's a part of who you are," he interrupted softly. "All the parts of you we've seen so far have been good. I don't agree with your faith, but I don't think it's bad either."

Holly nodded, drawing strength from her husband's consent and the knowledge that God had a plan for all of them. "I'm thanking the Lord for this dinner."

Emily and Jake's eyes went wide. Quickly, they looked at their father.

"It's alright. I didn't expect Holly to be just like me," Frank said. He looked at each of them and then continued, "I expect we will all have to make some adjustments. Holly comes from a different background, but she still agreed to come join our family. I'm sure we can all learn to get along with each other."

Frank's attitude seemed to have changed so much from this morning. While he was still unwilling to allow the Lord into his heart, something had softened him towards the idea. Holly was thankful for this. Faith was a personal relationship with the divine; Holly knew it could not be forced upon another, and that such a relationship would never be part of God's will. Still, this small step was significant. The smile, the joke, and now this...it was all leading to something. Holly began to hope that Frank was beginning to allow love into his heart once more.

"Thank you," Holly said with true gratitude. She bowed her head and shut her eyes and began, "We thank you Lord for this humble meal. Thank you for bringing us all together, for this fine home and family, for sustaining us with food. Thank you Lord for all your blessings."

Holly took a deep breath in and felt her heart fill with thanks. Yes, this was indeed a blessing. She felt nourished by her new family, warmed by sharing this food with them at the table. She dropped her head for a moment and dabbed her cloth against her cheek. Then she cut herself a bite of elk steak. "Emily, this is so delicious. I have never tasted elk before."

Jake laughed, "One day, dad is going to take me hunting. I promise to bring home a big one."

"That will be a proud day," said Holly. She gave Jake a big smile. He was so eager to grow up and be like his father.

"Emily will be an expert cook by then," Frank said.

"I don't know what all the fuss is about. It is just elk steak," said Emily.

"What's all this?" said Frank. He turned his head to face Emily. Emily twisted in her chair and tried not to look at him.

"It's alright," Holly said. "It has been a long day for us all."

Frank scowled, but said nothing more. Holly adjusted her grip on her fork, wishing they could find the peace and joy that had blessed them just a few minutes before. She knew she had to be patient. She and Emily had made great progress today, but they still had a long ways to go. Holly thanked God for the opportunity to see Emily without her veil of grief for a little while, and prayed for the strength to continue to help her on her path.

Emily ate greedily at first until the edge of her appetite was softened and then she pushed the last bits around on her plate with her fork. Emily watched her father and brother as they cleaned their plates and wiped them dry with the last of their biscuits. Emily seemed to make an effort not to look over in Holly's direction and remained quiet for the rest of the meal.

Holly was very aware that the child wouldn't look over at her. Emily probably needed more time.

The biscuits wanted a bit more leavening. Holly meant to apply herself to learn the ways of this particular stove. But she was pleased that there was a supply of bacon and eggs and butter, in the larder. The biscuits could do with a bit of jam as well. Tomorrow she would learn every inch of this household and explore the cellar. Perhaps she would find some dried fruit, then she could make a batch of jam.

Once the meal had ended, Holly pushed back her chair. It made a loud grating sound on the wooden floorboards. She chastened herself for making that racket. She said quietly to Emily, "Would you help me clear the table?"

Emily stared at her plate and acted as though she didn't hear Holly. Finally Frank spoke, "Emily you will clear the table as Holly asks."

Emily turned abruptly to her father but said nothing then made a great effort to scrape her chair legs along the floorboards much louder than Holly had.

Holly washed the dishes. Emily dried them with a sullen attitude. Jake played quietly and then went off to bed. Emily disappeared after sweeping the kitchen floor.

Patterns were already established. Something new had arrived but things stayed mostly just the same. The day wound down and soon everyone was to be in bed. If Holly wondered about that arrangement, there was no need. Frank stayed reading in his chair by the oil lamp light, stoking the fire and keeping the cold at bay. Holly straightened the coverlet and the sheets, plumped the pillows and fell asleep as soon as her head sunk into the stiff feather crinkle.

CHAPTER 6

Holly awoke, suddenly aware she was alone in the house. Where was everyone? Were they at work already? That wouldn't do. Even if it was her first full day on the farm as Frank Motherwell's wife, Holly had to pull her own weight. Quickly, she dressed, brushed her hair, and then braided it and wound it into a bun on top of her head.

She went to the kitchen and put a large kettle of water on to boil. She noted with satisfaction that the fire was well laid up and would burn for several hours. What this family needed was fresh bread.

She set out to make a sponge and laid that aside, covered with a dish towel, to rise on a shelf next to the stove. Once that was done, she allowed herself a moment of rest and glanced out the kitchen window. In the distance was Emily feeding the horses and Jake tending the pigs. She noticed that the bucket of peelings and the fat had been emptied.

From behind, she heard the front door open. Holly pushed herself from the counter and rubbed her palms on her dress. A moment later, she sighed. There was still some flour on them, and now that little bit of flour dusted the front of her garments. This wouldn't do. A hostess should be on point when welcoming a guest, but Holly didn't have time to fix it.

Taking a deep breath, she remembered Sister Maybelle's reassurances whenever she was a klutz or made a mistake with her chores at the orphanage: *You have a good heart, Holly, and that is what shines through and what people respond to—not appearances. Have faith in yourself and good things will come to you.*

Holly hoped Sister Maybelle was right.

The door opened. Frank, her new husband, stepped in. White winter sunlight spilled over his broad shoulders. He nodded when he saw her, not even seeing the flour on her skirt.

"Good morning," she said.

"Mornin'," he replied gruffly. "I have something for you." He went to the coat rack on the far side of the room, and picked out a pair of work that were lined up neatly against the wall beneath it.

"You'll be needing something more suitable for farm work," he explained. "Your city shoes are too fancy and too worn."

Holly quickly compared the sturdy boots in his hand to her "city shoes." They were simple and practical for work indoors or a quick stroll down a cobblestone street, but he was right. They would quickly wear out in the mud. Worse, she the lack of support for her ankles might result in injury. Holly had no doubt her husband would care for her if she was hurt, but she wanted to do everything possible to make sure she could help out while she was learning more about her position.

Frank handed her the boots. "They might be a little big for you, but they'll have to do for now. Next month, we can go into town and get you your own pair. They…belonged to Margaret," he added hesitantly.

Holly gripped the boots tightly. This must be a hard moment for Frank. She looked carefully in his face for signs of sentimentality but could find none.

"You can still wear your city shoes in the house, if you want. I guess now we should call them 'house shoes.'"

Holly nodded, smiling. "House shoes. I like it. That makes me sound rather dignified, does it not?"

Frank harrumphed, looking down at her flour-laden skirt. "Don't let it get to your head."

"Now you're just being silly," Holly replied as she unlaced her snug fitting thin leather boots and put on Margaret's more serviceable brogues."These 'house shoes' were hand-me-downs too, you know, from a kind patron of the orphanage. In fact, I own very few things that were not once someone else's."

Frank's expression grew somber. "We'll get you new shoes soon," he said softly.

Holly stood up straight. "I like it that way, actually," she corrected. She wasn't looking for pity, nor did she feel any pity for herself. "It reminds me of the goodwill of my neighbors. Charity is a gift and a virtue for both the giver and the receiver. It's a lesson I'll not forget every time I put on these boots." She wiggled her toes. They were perhaps a half size too large, but that wasn't anything a second pair of thick wool socks wouldn't fix.

Frank shook his head. "I hadn't thought about it quite that way, Holly. I'm glad the boots will do for now."

Holly grinned, grabbing a shawl. "They certainly will. Now, teach me how to manage the farm so I can help you properly."

Frank pointed at her skirt. "The first thing you must do is stop being self conscious about a little flour."

Holly gasped. "You could tell?"

"You have your hands in front of the spill like it's something to be ashamed of," Frank told her. "But you never have to be ashamed of your work, especially when you do it with all your heart."

Holly nodded, putting her hands at her sides. "Alright," he said, feeling lighter. Life on the farm sure was different than life back in Massachusetts, where her every movement was judged. Holly gave silent thanks that Sister Maybelle's kind words had truly come to pass.

Frank moved back to the front door. "As far as work goes, you had best learn from the children. Jake knows all about pigs and Emily knows horses. I suspect you know more than enough to fare in the kitchen, judging from those biscuits last night."

Holly nodded, pleased she would be able to spend more time with the children.

Frank opened the door. "Well, come with me. I'll show you the farm."

The wind was working at separating the last of the withered leaves from their weakening hold upon the trees. Holly wrapped her shawl tightly around her shoulders and tucked under its edges around her wrists.

Holly scanned the skies and thought ahead. Winter here would be harsh and a promise of snow cover for months. She gave a little thanks to God for giving Margaret slightly larger feet. This walk would be significantly less comfortable had her boots been pinching her toes, and as Frank had said, her own boots were woefully unsuited for these harsh high plains..

Soon they were at the barn. Frank drew back the large front door. Inside the smell of hay, manure and leather from harnesses and tack met her nose. The light was several shades reduced but additional light came from a dormer window at mid-roof.

"Come see how Emily and the mare are doing," Frank said as he led her to Daisy's stall.

Holly saw Emily stroking the mare's nose. The mare had big brown eyes and she was blowing and sniffing at Emily's hand.

Emily coaxed, "There Daisy, eat your hot mash. I made it just for you. You have to keep your strength up. Come on Daisy, I made it sweet. You'll love the extra molasses." Emily tore her eyes off Daisy for a moment to acknowledge Holly and her father. Then, she went back to stroking the mare and talking to her softly.

Daisy finally turned her attention from Emily's hand to the mash which steamed in her trough. Daisy's great swollen abdomen made her legs look spindly in comparison. Holly smiled at seeing Emily's concern and tenderness towards her mare.

"Come along, there's more to see on the farm," Frank said.

Once he'd led her away from Emily and Daisy, Holly asked, "Isn't it a little unusual for a mare to be foaling in late December?"

"It is indeed. A mare is pregnant for eleven months. Nature generally protects against winter births. Last fall was so unseasonably warm, there was no turn in weather to alert nature. I should have wondered when Daisy's winter coat didn't come in until January, and even then, it was sparse. Emily cinched a blanket around her, even before we figured she was pregnant."

Holly nodded, happy but not surprised by Emily's thoughtfulness and keen eye, for Emily had already shown Holly through her actions just how intelligent and kind she was. Again, Holly prayed that her relationship with the young girl could grow and blossom into a true friendship.

Maybe it could happen. Christmas was almost upon them, and though their quaint farm seemed as of yet untouched by the special holiday, miracles really could happen if one believed. Holly had witnessed numerous miracles firsthand at the orphanage—children finding good families, and hearts reopening to love. In fact, she was witnessing one now, for being blessed with the Motherwell family was nothing less than a miracle. Now, all she had to do was help Frank and his children to see that beauty was all around them, and that love was truly the greatest gift of all.

But first, breakfast. The sun was just beginning to rise, and the children would be hungry. In the future, she would wake before them to make sure their bellies were full before they started their chores.

Holly thanked Frank and then made her way back to the house. Putting on her 'house shoes,' she got to work.

The fresh bread was a hit at breakfast, especially when coupled with honey from the pantry. She also served porridge to make sure no tummies rumbled. After breakfast, everyone got up from the table and continued doing their chores.

Emily brought more hot mash to Daisy in the barn. Jake went out to check on the pigs. And Frank was going to check on the fence.

Having used up all the ingredients in the pantry the night before, Holly decided to go down to the root cellar and start looking for dinner. She took a basket from a hook in the kitchen and went down to the cellar.

It was little more than a closet sized room that contained ice, straw, and wood shavings. Still, it preserved things for quite a while if they were wrapped in muslin and then buried in the chips and covered with snow and bits of ice. She rummaged in the straw and picked out three potatoes, she went to another area and picked out an onion and a couple of carrots. She went to the crock and pulled out a slab of salted pork. After drying her hands on her apron, she picked up her basket and came back up the stairs.

Holly filled the large iron kettle with water and roughly chopped the vegetables. Then, she rinsed the slab of pork in several changes of water. Finally, she chopped up the pork and added it to the kettle, put on the lid, and left her soup on the outer edge of the stove to simmer for the next several hours.

Now that dinner was taken care of, she went outside and sought out Frank. He was just outside the barn, unloading grain off the wagon.

"It is less than a week before Christmas," Holly said after he grunted a greeting.

Frank frowned. "Is that so?" he asked, continuing his work.

"Yes, and I think it would be nice for the children to have a tree," Holly continued.

Frank stopped his work and crossed his arms over his chest.

Oh dear. She didn't like the sour expression that was crossing his face. Was she stepping out of line? Holly didn't think so; her husband was a reasonable man, so she needed to be clear so he knew where she was coming from. "A Christmas tree doesn't have to be a symbol of religiosity," Holly explained. "Rather, it is a symbol of friendship and new beginnings."

As expected, Frank had his own opinions. "We have done just fine without a tree for Christmas a few years now. Seems a waste of a good tree and means an afternoon without work. No need for that foolery," he said in his measured, gravelly voice.

But Holly wasn't so easily dissuaded. "What if the children finish their chores?"

Frank cocked his head to the side. "What are you getting at?"

"I mean, would you let us take the wagon and Buck if the children and I finish our work?"

Frank shook his head. "I don't see any problem with that. If all of you want to rush so you can waste your time with this fruitless task, then that is your business. But I don't think they'll want a tree."

Aha! Holly thought. "Well, I'll ask them, if it's alright with you."

"It's fine, but I'm telling you you're wasting your time," Frank muttered, then got back to work.

Holly had been dismissed, but her heart was soaring. She knew the children would want a Christmas tree, and even more than that, she knew this family needed Christmas. Now that she'd received Frank's blessing, nothing could stop her.

CHAPTER 7

First, Holly had to find the children. Holly was easy to find. Though the little girl was slightly reluctant to leave Daisy, but her eyes lit up when Holly explained that her absence would be due to finding a Christmas tree.

"Is it alright with father?" the small girl asked.

"Yes, your father said it was alright," Holly reassured.

"Oh, that's so great!" Emily exclaimed as the infectious light returned to her eyes.

Holly smiled. "Now, let's go find your brother. We will need him to cut it down for us."

Jake beamed when Holly asked him. He couldn't wait to get the chance to be a man and chop down his first tree with a hatchet, and finished feeding the pigs in double time. He even helped his father unload the grain from the wagon. Then, Jake brought Buck around and harnessed him to the wagon. Before they left, Frank insisted they all put on another layer of clothing for the foothills had snow.

Holly had never seen two children more eager to obey their father. Frank was taken aback as well. "It's just a tree," he muttered as Holly and the kids bundled into the wagon.

But nothing can dampen infectious Christmas spirit. Jake clicked his tongue and flicked the reins.

The small party headed east. The low hills had evergreens, there they were certain to find a suitable tree. Holly smiled as both children snuggled against her. Jake skillfully handled the reins as Emily sat peaceably beside her in the wagon's bench seat.

"I want a real tall tree!" Jake told them.

"But we have a small home," said Emily. "We should get a small tree."

Holly chuckled. Jake was so full of enthusiasm, and Emily was endearingly practical. "Let's look for something full and fluffy," Holly said. "Oh, it will smell divine!"

Soon the road ended and they tied up Buck and let him look for sprigs of grain stalks poking out of the snow. They trudged up a low incline and scattered to see if there was a proper tree to cut.

"I've found it!" Emily called out.

Holly and Jake came quickly. Emily had found a glade of mixed alder and maple trees. Standing between them was a nine foot tall noble fir.

Jake nodded. "This will do," he said, then got to work clearing the snow at the base of the trunk. Emily and Holly stood back, watching him go. This seemed to suit Jake fine. After procuring the hatchet, he started whacking the trunk as if he were butchering it.

"Take off a few lower limbs to give yourself some room to work," Holly offered. She wished they had brought a saw but the only one Frank had was three feet long and Holly feared that would cause an accident if they tried to wield it. The hatchet would just have to do.

After a few minutes of solid hard work, Jake got through the middle and then a few strokes later, the tree fell into the snow.

Jake and Emily laughed and fell over in the snow themselves. Holly laughed in spite of herself. "Come on," she said, pulling them to their feet. Then, she dusted off the snow from their clothes.

The hard work wasn't over yet, though. They all did their part to bring the tree back to the wagon. Each grabbed a branch and dragged it.

Perhaps they had begun later than was wise. By the time they got back to the wagon, the sky was lowering with grey clouds and Holly could hear Jake's stomach give a rumble. They each hoisted the tree trunk first down the length of the wagon and climbed aboard the buckram. Jake once again clicked his tongue and shook the reins. Buck immediately started homeward.

"Let's sing a carol. Do you know Deck The Halls?" Holly asked.

Emily frowned. "No."

"Jingle Bells?" Holly ventured.

"Everybody knows that one!" Emily replied.

"Yeah," Jake agreed in a grunt reminiscent of his father's.

"Good. Then let's sing!" Before they had time to protest, Holly began.

At first, Holly thought she'd be singing all alone, but by the time she got to the chorus Jake joined in. Emily did soon after in a voice so sweet and pure that Holly was pleased to be seated right beside her. Why, Emily had the voice of an angel. Why didn't she sing just for the pleasure of hearing her own voice?

When they were done with the song, Holly said, "That was wonderful. I had no idea how musical you both are. It is a shame that you don't sing more."

Jake tucked his chin down and said, under his breath, "We don't sing much since momma died."

"Especially carols," Emily added quietly.

Jake nodded. "Father doesn't want to hear any singing and asked us not to bring those church songs into the house."

Holly's heart broke for her husband. The pain of Frank's loss had isolated him from many of the wonderful things in life that could bring him joy. She wished there was some way she could ease his pain, but Frank seemed to nurture it, coddle it, keep it safe from the light of day and even from fresh air. It was a sorrow that had burrowed in like a worm and ate at the core of an apple.

It was hard to expel such pain. Frank had no doubt grown accustomed to it. He'd probably even begun to depend on it. His sorrow was proof that his wife and lived and that he had loved her. Holly worried whether anyone could get him to let a little light shine into his heart and show him some peace.

"Singing is good for the soul and good exercise for the mind and body. I would like to have us practice some songs for you to sing on Christmas," Holly said.

"Singing is only done in church and father won't set foot in church," said Jake.

Holly recalled Frank's impatience and brittleness while they were in church. Was his great loss the source of it? Had his sorrow turned to anger against God? Holly began to understand his behavior a little better—especially since he'd been in that church to marry her, which he might have seen as yet another betrayal.

Holly refused to allow her shoulders to slump. "Well, that may be so, but we can still have a nice dinner together on Christmas Eve. We can enjoy the trimmed tree and light some extra candles. Then, on Christmas morning, open presents."

"We don't have any presents," said Jake

"Father doesn't believe in Christmas presents," said Emily softly. "Not since mom died."

"Well, we don't have to worry about what St. Nicholas brings. We will make do ourselves," Holly decided. "Christmas presents do not have to be elaborate to be meaningful. I'm sure each of you knows what the other one wants. I think there's a way for you to make that happen. For instance, Emily, your father has holes in his socks. I'll bet you could darn them up and give them to him on Christmas day. Jake, you know your father has been asking for you to finish getting the rust off and oiling the plow. Maybe that is a project you could work on, without him noticing. Then, you could show him your work on Christmas day."

There was a brief silence.

"I guess that would be alright," Jake said finally, breaking it. "Father has been asking me about that a lot. He'd appreciate me doing it."

Emily said nothing but snuggled up against Holly, shivering. Holly put her arm around Emily, and the young girl did not reject her offer of comfort. Luckily, they were close to home. Buck's pace had increased, and the outline of the farm could be seen.

When the wagon pulled up, Frank appeared immediately. His usual long strides were quicker and heavier and he wore a frown. Holly thought he looked like he might blow smoke and roar.

"What is the matter?" asked Holly.

"You shouldn't be out in the woods until dark. Don't you know something could have happened to you?" Frank growled. "Holly, I would expect that you would have taken better care of them." Frank grabbed the reins and unfastened Buck from his wagon. He looked dangerously angry and Holly wasn't quite sure what to say. She and the children quickly climbed down from the buckram.

"We were fine. I assure you we were safe," Holly said once her footing was steady.

Frank shut his eyes. "I'm sorry I raised my voice. I was just worried for a moment. I...I want you all to be careful when you go out is all. I should have gone with you. I don't know why I didn't. Next time, I will."

"Next time you'll come with us to find a Christmas tree?" Emily asked.

Frank looked at her strangely as if shocked by the hope in her voice. "I suppose I will."

"Father, look at the fine tree we brought back," said Jake.

Frank took a look at it and pulled it off the wagon in one fell swoop and dropped it, trunk down, into the horse trough. "This is big. How did you get it in the cart?"

"We all worked together," Emily said.

"That you did," Frank murmured.

"I chopped it down myself," Jake told his father proudly.

Frank tousled Jake's hair. "You brought back a nice tree. I wish I could have seen it."

Jake smiled up at his father.

Frank sighed, back to business. "Well, the tree will need water to stay fresh if you want it to last until Christmas. I suppose since you've all gone to the trouble of getting it I can do my part. It's too late to get it set up now, but it will last for a while outside. We can deal with it in a few days."

"Your father is right, children," Holly said. "Let's get it set up and then decorated. Oh, it will look so beautiful and smell so lovely and fresh!"

Frank raised his eyebrows and gave Holly a quick look. "Is that so?"

Holly wrung her hands together, suddenly self conscious. "Yes. You won't have to do a thing, just let us have our fun."

"Fine," Frank acquiesced, "as long as no one takes the wagon and goes out in the woods without supervision again."

"I hope you didn't miss us too badly while we were gone," Holly said with a smile.

"I'll put the horse away. You all look wet. Go in and change before you catch cold," Frank's words might have been gruff, but his concern was evident to Holly.

"Come in the house you two, we will get you warm and dry," Holly said. "Dinner will be at the usual time, so don't be too long putting away the wagon."

Once inside the house they all stripped off their outer layers. Holly noted that Frank had already laid fresh logs in the stove and the house was piping warm. She lifted the lid of the large iron kettle and saw that the pork stew was nicely done. It was lucky that she had left the soup on the edge of the stove. Now all that remained to do for dinner was to make quick biscuits.

By the time Frank had come inside, the kitchen smelled rich and fragrant. Emily and Jake had already set the table, so all that was left to do was sit down and enjoy a hearty meal after a full day's work.

CHAPTER 8

The next morning Holly made sure to wake before anyone else. Swiftly, she prepared breakfast, happy that they'd all now start their day on the right foot. After a breakfast of eggs and leftover biscuits, Frank and Jake got up went outside to tend to the animals. Emily and Holly were left to clear away the table.

Holly immediately noticed a change in the young girl. Instead of picking up a few plates and then shying away, Emily grabbed the broom and gave the main floor a careful sweep while Holly washed the dishes. Emily then hung the broom up from its nail on the wall and came over to Holly. Picking up a clean cloth, she dried the washed dishes.

Holly sensed that something was coming. She held her tongue and waited for Emily to speak.

"I was thinking about your suggestion of, well, about your idea of Christmas presents," Emily began hesitantly. "I'd like to fix father's socks properly. They have horrible holes in the heel and toes. I doubt they even keep his feet warm. But the problem is, I don't know how to do it." As Emily admitted this last bit, she lowered her eyes in shame.

"I'm not sure I knew how to darn socks before your age, either," said Holly. "I could teach you in a few minutes. Just remember, it is a skill that you perfect with practice. It might go slowly at first, but soon you can practically do it in your sleep. Come, sit down at the table and I'll get my needles and yarn."

Holly returned with her personal bag that she had brought with her from the orphanage. She hadn't opened it in such a long time that memories of Sister Maybelle flooded in while she spread out her treasures. Smiling, Holly picked up a silver thimble that neatly fit the middle finger. She placed this on Emily's right hand explaining, "This is for pushing the end of the needle through thick fabric. It saves your finger so much wear."

"It's just beautiful," Emily held up her hand and admired the thimble on her finger, twisting her hand from all angles.

"That looks like it fits you pretty well," Holly said. When had Sister Maybelle given it to her? She must have been about Holly's age. She remembered it fitting her finger similarly.

"Now," Holly began, "these large sewing needles are specially made for darning. See the huge eye of the needle? The next size down is for embroidery. But we will use the needles for darning today."

Emily nodded, completely focused on Holly's instruction.

Holly then selected a dark brown wool skein. "The last thing we need is a pair of scissors." She brought out a delicate pair of scissors that looked like a silver stork. The snipping ends were the long bill of the bird, hinged at the eye. They formed a slight curve and widened gradually to suggest the neck and breast of the bird. They were fullest at the body, that split at the legs which ended in a pair of rounded handles. The largest round handle had just the trace of a tail.

Emily gave an inadvertent sigh when she saw those beautiful scissors. Holly placed them in her hand and Emily marveled at how effortlessly and soundlessly they worked.

"Whoever gave you such a treasure?" Emily asked.

"They were given to me by Sister Maybelle, from the orphanage."

"What a funny name. Surely she must have loved you the most of all her girls. I never knew scissors could be so beautiful."

"How nice of you to say that. I suppose Sister Maybelle did have a soft spot for me. She was always so careful to treat us all the same. But when I left she insisted that I take her very own scissors and sewing bag to remember her by." Holly hoped that Emily didn't notice the catch in her throat, or the fact that she had to blink several times to clear her eyes.

"So, you'll want to stuff the sock with a rounded piece of wood," Holly continued. "Sister Maybelle had a wooden 'egg' which she shoved into the toe or heel of the sock. It gives you a form to guide the stitches and prevents you from accidentally sewing the toes together, making the sock even smaller. Let's see. I suppose we could use the end of a wooden spoon."

After that explanation, Holly stood. She was grateful for the opportunity to get up and move, and quickly dabbed her eye with the edge of her apron as she had her back turned. Once her eyes were once again dry, she returned with the spoon and continued the lesson.

"Here we go," she began. "Now, Spoon in. Thread the needle. Yes, that's right. Here, let me show you how to begin." Holly doubled the yarn to about a foot long. "Will you snip it for me please, right there?"

Emily gingerly picked up the scissors. Taking care to keep her thimble on her third finger, she snipped it and a bright smile broke over her face.

"That is fine. Now I make a knot at the end of this and then begin sewing a rather open pattern of parallel lines. Here, now you continue what I have begun until you get to the other side of the hole."

Holly handed the sock over to Emily who began to breathe in quick shallow breaths.

"There is nothing to worry about. You cannot ruin these socks. Remember, we are mending. What can be done can be undone. Well, unless you take the scissors to the sock."

Emily gave a little smile and then her face became serious again. Tentatively, the little girl took a little stitch into the bottom of the hole and then drew the needle and thread across the gap and just as she tried to get the needle to come back out again, she dropped it.

Holly understood Emily's frustration before she gave voice to it. "At first it feels foreign and your fingers feel like they are all thumbs. But soon there will be a rhythm and it all becomes second nature."

Emily kept her head bent and eyes focused making her needle do as she was told. Soon, she had made a dozen parallel stitches and crossed the gap.

"That looks fine," Holly said, proud of Emily's work. "What you are going to do now is to turn the sock 90 degrees and come back across those stitches. Now comes the fun part. You can dip the needle over and under those stitches, and alternate when you come back. In this way, you are building a weave. It is strong and keeps the sock from bunching. You wouldn't want your socks to have a knot or a bump at the heel or toe. This will all work to make a smooth patch."

Emily continued to work away at her task. Holly watched her and thought this must have been how Sister Maybelle had felt when teaching Holly the same lesson long ago. She remembered how awkward and complex it had felt at the beginning. Then, suddenly it was all ease and even pleasurable to accomplish any sewing task.

"There, you've got it," Holly murmured. "Now, let the needle fall and test your work. Do you see any places you have missed?"

"I think I see a gap there." Emily pointed to the spot with a discouraged voice.

"Then that is where you will go through once more. You can give the sock another turn, perhaps at forty-five degrees. When you can get to the other side, just tie off the stitching."

Holly instructed Emily how to make a couple back stitches and leave a little loop and thread the needle through and pull it tight and make a knot.

"Don't cut it too closely," Holly warned. "Take another shallow stitch, kind of slide your needle through the sock and come out about the length of the needle away. Now snip the thread. See? You have buried the end and it will look and hold better."

Emily did as she was told and looked back at Holly expectantly.

Holly smiled. "What a fine job. I don't think my first sock went quite so well. You are quick learner."

Emily's eyes lit up, her face softened and the corners of her mouth turned up slightly.

At that moment, there was a sound at the door. Frank entered the house. Emily gave an involuntary gasp and quickly buried the evidence of her new lesson beneath her apron.

"What are you two doing?" he asked.

"N-nothing!" Emily stammered.

Frank frowned. "That won't do."

"I assure you we were not being idle. We're doing women's work," Holly said. "What are *you* doing?"

Frank raised his brows, taken aback by Holly's sassy tone. Holly winced, wishing she could take it back, but she didn't want to ruin Emily's surprise!

"Well, I have just come in for hot water," Frank explained. "Jake has taken over Emily's duty of making hot mash for Daisy."

"Well, that sounds nice," Holly replied.

Frank's scowl returned. He didn't look angry, more befuddled at finding Emily and Holly sitting together at the table. Frank gave both of them a questioning look.

Emily broke the silence, "I will bring out the water. Tell Jake I have not forgotten Daisy's hot mash. It will be right out."

"Alright then. But you two are acting mighty mysterious," Frank said.

"No we're not!" Emily squeaked, making a sound that could, unfortunately, only be described as mighty mysterious.

Frank shook his head. "Well, you'll both be happy to know I don't have time to question you. There's a lot to get done before Christmas this year."

Emily and Holly glanced at each other. He didn't know how right he was!

With that, Frank turned and went right back out the door.

"Alright, how quickly can we bring that water up to a boil?" Emily whispered. She looked at Holly and suddenly they broke into laughter.

CHAPTER 9

The next day, the temperature dropped into the low twenties. Outside chores were limited to feeding the farm animals, gathering eggs and milking the cows. Frank couldn't get much done without harnessing the horse and wagon. It was useless to try anyway. He wouldn't risk injuring Buck pulling a wagon from town and back. He gave everyone leave to stay inside for the day. Surely tomorrow it would be more hospitable.

Holly didn't have to worry about what was going to keep Emily occupied. She had seen Emily gather the rag basket and the sewing bag and head back to her bedroom and shut the door. However, Jake was another matter. He sat at the table, wiggling his legs and looking dreamily out the window. She spied a block of wood in the kindling box. She walked over to him and quietly asked if he knew how to whittle.

"Of course. I have handled a knife since I was five," he assured her.

"Well then, I need your help on a project. Can you to make us a nice round shaped oval out of this block. Keep it mostly the same size, just round out the edges. After you do that, it needs to be sanded smooth as silk. Do you think you could do that?"

Jake took the block of wood out of Holly's hand. "Of course I could. It might take me a few hours but I could do it."

"Could you just work quietly on this project? I happen to know that Emily needs an object just like this. Why, you could even give it to her for Christmas. It would make a very nice present. Would you like to do that?" Holly asked innocently.

Jake's expression turned thoughtful. "I was wondering what to get her. Do you think she is gonna give me a present?"

Holly smiled. "Yes, I'm sure she's going to give you something for Christmas."

The boy grinned from ear to ear. He walked to the stove and took out a buck knife from a tin box. Then, he moved his chair over to the fire and began to whittle away little strips of wood. Soon, a nice little pile had gathered at his feet.

Frank was seated in a chair reading. Every once in awhile his eyes peeped over the pages to watch their exchange.

The house was quiet and Holly had a pot of soup going on the stove. She took a moment to envision where the tree would stand in the room. Closing her eyes, she inhaled deeply and imagined how the house would smell like green like sap.

Her eyes whipped open. Wait, how would they decorate it? There were no glass ornaments, nor any little candles that one could clamp onto the branches.

Holly's first Christmas at the orphanage had been the first Christmas she could remember. She wasn't certain how Sister Maybelle had managed to convince her uncle to let her run the old, rundown tenement house in a rough part of town, but she had. At the age of five, she'd joined four other children who took shelter there under Sister Maybelle's care.

That first Christmas, Sister Maybelle told them that they were the luckiest children of all. Other children had their trees come ready-made. Theirs was to be created from what was at hand.

Then, Sister Maybelle sat them at a table with a long piece of twine and a needle. In front of them were two big bowls: one filled with cranberries, the other filled with popcorn.

Holly remembered trying to thread her needle through the cranberries, but they were slippery. She'd stabbed her finger more than once, and her hands had become stained with cranberry juice and perhaps a few drop of blood. Sister Maybelle suggested that she thread popcorn instead.

Holly remembered doing this for a while, but then she tired of the project and just ate the popcorn. First she ate all the broken pieces that scattered in front of her, and then she ate every third piece of popcorn. Soon, though, all she did was smile and watch the older children at work, happily eating popcorn and humming along as they sang Christmas Carols. That first Christmas had also been her happiest.

Holly smiled as she realized that the Motherwell tree could be strewn with paper chains and long strands of popcorn. Their tree could be beautiful, even without ornaments and lights.

"Did I catch you wool gathering?" Frank's voice was just behind her.

Holly gave a little jump and spun around, flushing with exasperation.

"I didn't mean to startle you," he said quickly. "I was struck with the look of your face just now. Were you thinking fondly of something? I wanted to know what it was."

Right after he said this, he dipped his head down and glanced at the wood stove. Holly suddenly got the impression that he'd rather be stoking the fire instead of getting tangled up with her thoughts.

"Yes, I guess I was. I was imagining where to put the Christmas tree and how it will be decorated."

Frank brushed his hand through his brown hair. It immediately sprung back over his forehead again. He had a boyish sort of hair that wouldn't behave. "I'm not sure the children care either way. We haven't had the need of a tree in several years. I don't think

Jake was even old enough to remember having one. But, since you went out for a tree and Jake cut it down, I expect I can make a stand for it and set it where you'd like."

"Thank you," Holly said. "I think the tree would look well in the corner, near the front window."

"That would be a fine spot for it. You know, a tree is thirsty. I think it should be in a bucket and then the stand would set around that."

"You think of everything. Could you make such a stand?" Holly asked, suddenly warmed by the fact Frank had offered to help.

"Jake and I can rig something along those lines. It will work but I can't guarantee it will be pretty," he said.

"It will be pretty, no matter if you place it in a commode," Holly replied before she realized quite what she had said.

Frank's eyes grew wide.

Holly giggled.

"In any event, it will bring in the smell of sap and greens and will be magical."

All of a sudden Frank's face fell, "Then the children will expect presents. I don't often go to town and never shop beyond necessities."

"Don't you worry. I have the children working on their own presents. Jake is making something for Emily, Emily is making something for you. That leaves you to think of something for Jake."

Frank gave her a quiet look. Scratching behind his head, he said, "But that leaves you out of rotation."

"I have received more than I expected already. I just want us to have a real Christmas."

"That isn't enough," Frank whispered. "You cannot do so much for other people, and yet expect nothing for yourself."

Holly sucked in a breath, unsure of how to proceed. He had given her so much already. In fact, all of the Motherwell's had. Each day with them was a gift, didn't they see that?

"Holly?" he prompted.

She exhaled slowly. "I truly am grateful for this life you have chosen to share with me, Frank Motherwell. This time last year, I feared I would have to spend the rest of my Christmases alone. Sister

Maybelle and the others would have always welcomed me, yes, but I did not want to impose on them. And also, there was a deeper, selfish reason. I wanted, more than anything, to have a true home of my own."

Frank said nothing. Holly's heart pounded furiously in her chest. She knew that he viewed their relationship as purely functional and that he did not want to allow her into his heart. Opening up like this made her vulnerable, and, more importantly, imposed on Frank's generosity.

"I do not mean to make you uncomfortable, Frank," Holly added quickly. "I knew what I was getting into when I accepted your offer. I just want you to know that it is more than satisfactory. In fact, it is more than I wished for."

Frank sighed. "That just makes me feel worse, Holly, because it isn't much. A girl like you..." he shut his eyes. "A girl like you," he began again, "deserves more than that."

Holly was surprised at the sudden heat flooding her cheeks. Was she blushing? She touched her cheek, finding it surprisingly warm. Yes, she *was* blushing. Oh dear. Thankfully, Frank wasn't looking at her!

As soon as she had that thought, his deep blue eyes rose to meet hers once more. Holly suddenly felt as hot as a squealing teapot.

"What do you want for Christmas, Holly?" he asked.

Holly did not know what to say, and for a moment, she did not even know if she could speak. The way he looked at her made her tummy feel rather strange. The strangest thing about this feeling, though, was the fact that she sort of liked it.

This time it was her turn to shut her eyes during her response. "There is something that I do want, but it is a selfish wish," she began honestly. "More than that, it is something I promised you I would not speak of. Please, do not ask me again and tempt me to break my promise."

"What is it?" he asked.

"What did I just tell you?" Holly stammered. She tried to be good, but she did not have limitless willpower.

"I am asking you what you want, Holly Motherwell," he said softly.

Holly gasped. That was the first time she'd ever heard him refer to her as a Motherwell.

"I do not want you to hide something like this from me," he continued. "So no matter what it is, I want to hear it, even if it is something that I previously said I did not want to hear. Holly, what do you want for Christmas?"

Holly's heart soared. His kind words meant so much to her. Did he really mean them? Did she have the strength to speak them?

Holly prayed to God silently to give her the strength to ask for her true wish, knowing that if it were to come to pass it would truly be a Christmas miracle. Taking a deep breath, she surrendered to His power, trusting Him that He gave her this opportunity to guide them both. "Alright then. I would like, more than anything this Christmas, to go to church."

Frank frowned, but said nothing. Slowly, he turned away from her and walked back to his book.

Holly couldn't move. What did his sudden departure mean? Had she upset him? Had she done something wrong? She put her hand over her swiftly beating heart, trying to steady it, but it would not steady. Too many emotions were coursing through her. Confusion. Fear. Hope.

Yes, hope.

No matter what the future held for her, Holly had faith in the Lord and His will. He chose to bring her here, and she had to believe He had a plan and a good reason. Christmas truly was the season of miracles. Frank, who was so hard-working and so capable of love, deserved one.

Holly closed her eyes and made her Christmas wish. It was one that was filled with faith and family and, most of all, love.

CHAPTER 10

The heavy winds did not subside until the sun was beginning to set, leaving the last light of day bitterly cold. Holly looked up at the pink and turquoise sky over her soup. She saw Jake was working on a very rounded out piece of wood. She walked back to Emily's room and knocked quietly.

"Emily, it's probably time for Daisy's hot mash. You'll want to get back from the barn before it gets dark."

"Oh, thanks. I've been darning socks. They are nearly all done," Emily whispered.

"You are probably an expert by now," Holly noted. "Your father is asleep, I want you to come out quietly and not disturb him."

Holly then walked over to Jake and leaned over his shoulder. "That's fine work you are doing. It is time to go out and do your evening chores. If you leave the house quietly, your father might get to sleep until supper."

Jake looked up, his mouth and eyes opened wide. Sure enough, Frank was sprawled out in his chair with his head off to the side, covering his eyes with the back of his forearm. Jake gave Holly a conspiratorial smile and quietly bundled up along with Emily. They shut the front door with a minimum of sound. Holly gave them both a wink while Frank continued to sleep.

By the time supper was ready, Emily and Jake had returned from their errands. After taking off their coats, the children huddled around the stove trying to warm their frozen hands.

A gust of cold wind and noise of the door closing woke Frank. He blinked as if he were in a daze, and his face was flushed pink. Clearly he was not in the habit of napping.

"Why did you let me sleep?" Frank asked no one in particular.

"It looked like you needed some rest," Holly said.

"Did all the chores get done?" Frank asked.

"All done." "Yes." Emily and Jake chorused.

Frank still didn't look fully satisfied. He was the kind of man who loathed to rest until everything that needed doing was finished. Holly respected that, but also understood that such men often needed rest the most.

"Alright children, wash up and come to supper. I don't want these biscuits getting cold," Holly said in a mock bossy tone. Then, she winked at the children who could barely contain their giggles, for Frank's unexpected nap had a secondary benefit: it had allowed Emily and Jake to work on their presents for him undisturbed.

By the time she'd laid the table everyone was in their chairs. Holly sat down and spread out her napkin on her lap. Jake reached for a biscuit before Frank's voice cut him off.

"Not yet, Jake."

Jake looked up, confused. "What's wrong?"

Frank leveled a gaze at Holly.

Holly squirmed in her seat. What did *she* do?

"We must wait until Holly says grace," Frank said.

Holly was so stunned she couldn't speak.

"Well?" Frank prompted.

"I...I thought..." Holly stammered.

Frank lowered his eyes as if ashamed. "It's not quite church, but it's something, isn't it?" he asked softly.

Holly's heart grew warm. Was Frank meeting her halfway?

At that moment, Jake's stomach growled. "Oh, please say grace Holly! I'm so hungry!"

Holly couldn't help but smile. When she was as young as Jake, she'd also thought grace was just an unnecessary step between her and her much desired meal. It wasn't until she was older that she understood the true benefit of saying thanks. Now, she was able to share that gift with this family.

Holly shut her eyes and lowered her head. "Lord," she began, "we thank you for this day of rest and work, and for providing us a warm and safe home during the storm. We thank you for the wonderful food upon this table. Most of all, we thank you for giving us each other."

With that, she looked up with a smile.

"Can we eat yet?" Jake asked.

Holly laughed. "Wait a moment, Jake. I would like each of us to go around the table and say something we are thankful for."

Jake tried to stifle his groan, but failed. Emily, however, took the lead.

"I'm thankful for Daisy," Emily said. "She is such a wonderful horse, and I'm sorry she's going through a tough time. I like bringing her mush. I hope she will be okay."

"Daisy will be fine," Frank said. "And I'm sure if she could talk, she would be thankful for you for bringing her mush."

Emily smiled sweetly at her father.

"What about me?" Jake asked.

Emily glared at her brother. "What do you mean?"

"Aren't you thankful for me?" Jake asked.

Emily rolled her eyes. "Fine. *And* Jake. Sort of."

"What is that supposed to mean?" Jake asked.

"Come on you two," Frank interjected. "Maybe you should go next, Jake."

Jake nodded, suddenly somber. "I'm thankful for the tree I chopped down myself. And for Holly and Emily and Buck for coming out with me. And for father for helping us get the tree off the wagon."

"Oh, I'm thankful for Holly too," Emily interrupted. Then, her cheek went pink, as if she was startled by what she'd just said. "And father. And

Buck. And the tree. The tree is going to be so pretty when father puts it up," she added softly.

"It certainly will," Frank said.

There was a moment of silence as all three waited, wondering if Frank was going to join in. With a heavy sigh, he murmured. "I suppose it's my turn. I'm thankful to see Emily and Jake smile again. And though I don't understand it, and it's just going to be more work, I'm thankful for that tree, because I'm pretty sure that tree has something to do with their good mood."

Then, he looked up at Holly. "But most of all, I'm glad that Holly was the one who answered my letter, because ham hock and white bean soup is my favorite and boy can she cook."

Holly felt another blush blooming on her cheeks.

Jake was oblivious to her discomfort, "Amen!" he said.

Holly's eyes went wide. Emily giggled.

"What?" Jake asked. "Isn't it time to eat?"

"Yes, son," Frank laughed. His bright eyes rose across the table to meet Holly's, and this time they did not look away. "Let's enjoy this beautiful meal."

Chapter 11

The next day was still bitterly cold. Yesterday's storm had left the ground covered with a dusting of snow, light as feathers. After Frank and Jake finished their chores, Jake came in and took the rifle off the wall. He flashed a smile at Emily and Holly and dashed back outdoors. It was a miracle the boy could see beneath the brim of his father's hat. Jake could use a stocking cap. So could Frank, for that matter.

Holly went to her green velvet bag with the bone handle. She gathered a couple skeins of wool and two circular needles. "Emily, would you like a lesson in how to knit?"

Emily came right over and together they sat upon the sofa near the stove. Holly divided her supplies and then began, "The first thing you'll need to know is how to cast on your stitches." Holly's fingers were nimble and quick, making looping motions around the tip of the needle and repeating them until she had made half a dozen. Then she handed the needle and yarn to Emily and let her try to do the same. Emily's fingers were unsure and stiff, but she cast on one and then another loops. "This is harder than it looks. What if I make a mistake?" she worried aloud.

"No matter," Holly said softly. "Knitting is very forgiving. You can always unravel and correct a mistake. All you need to do is pay close attention for a while and then suddenly the movements become second nature."

Emily continued making loops around her needle, splaying the thread between the fingers of her left hand.

"There, you've got enough now," Holly said as she took the needle from Emily. "Now I can show you how to knit." Holly took the needles in one hand and threaded the yarn around her index finger and trailed the slack around her pinky finger. "So, now enter the cast-on stitch, crossing below with the left hand needle's tip. With your left index finger, throw an extra loop around that stitch. See how the needle tips are crossing and the left hand needle looks like there are two stitches there? Now, as you slightly raise the tip of the needle in your left hand, you slowly retract your right hand. These are small movements, just enough to transfer over the doubled yarn. I know it looks and sounds complicated but just watch me make a few stitches."

Emily watched Holly's fingers so closely that Holly felt Emily's warm breath upon her hands.

"Alright, now I am going to hand this over for you to practice. Remember, there is nothing that can go wrong that can't be made right. At first it feels very strange, but trust me, you will soon have your needles flying and see that this can be such fun," Holly said. She handed over the circular affair, and showed Emily where to hold the needles. She threaded the yarn through Emily's left hand and instructed her step by step in what she should do. Patiently, she repeated the same instructions. Again and again, she helped Emily guide her needle into the stitches in the pattern of passing one needle beneath and adding a loop of thread and then slipping that stitch onto the left hand's needle again and again. Emily's confidence grew, even if she forgot what came next, Holly gently reminded her or guided her hand. With repetition, which was the essence of knitting, Emily's hands gradually became committed to the pattern. Then she was knitting all on her own. Holly waited until Emily finished a whole row without the need of a prompt or reminder.

"You have it. You are knitting. That's all there is to it. Look how far you've come," Holly pointed to Emily's progress. "Your hat is two inches long!"

Emily looked from her knitting and back to Holly. Her eyes shone with pride and her smile widened. She turned back to her knitting and her index finger kept plying the thread while her needles met and separated with regularity.

Holly smiled to herself and began making another hat herself. Soon they were both stitching away happily, heads down, hands full of industry. They made a bit of small talk and before they knew it, the daylight altered and it was afternoon.

"Look, I've made such progress. You can tell it's a hat!" Emily exclaimed. "I think this one will be for father."

"It is excellently made. Then mine will be for Jake." Holly replied. "But where are they? They have been gone for quite some time."

Just at that moment Holly could hear Buck give a whiney. She looked out the window and saw Frank and Jake tramping back to the house. Frank had the rifle cracked over his shoulder and Jake held a bundle of something slung over his shoulder as well. Holly imagined how cold they must be. She got up and quickly went to the stove and added another log. She filled a kettle with water and set it on the heat for tea just as she heard their footsteps on the porch.

They burst into the house with a gust of cold wind and a small flurry of feathery down snow.

"You must be nearly frozen, you two," Holly exclaimed.

"I shot a snowshoe rabbit," Jake cried out. "First we spotted his tracks and then I saw him hopping. I got him on the second shot."

"Let's warm up our hands for a minute and then you and I will go back out and flay him and we will have the best rabbit stew you've ever eaten," Frank said as he patted Jake proudly on his back.

Jake handed off the limp rabbit to Holly who, without thinking, clung to its hind legs and dangled upside down from her hand. Frank looked at her and gave a laugh, "It looks like you've never held a rabbit before. Have you ever cooked one?"

"No, but I imagine they aren't much different than chicken," Holly said with a stunned and blank look on her face.

"No, not so much different than chicken. Except they have a whole lot of little bones. We are all in for a rare treat," Frank said with a wide smile covering his face.

Holly continued to stare at him and then became aware that she was still holding the rabbit's hind legs. She must look a sight. She turned and hastily laid the long white creature upon the counter. It's body was pliable and the white fur was so soft. Her hand absently stroked it. She looked up and Jake was busy warming his hands at the stove and stamping his feet to get the blood moving again. Frank gave her a curious look and then turned and joined Jake at the stove.

"Get out of your wet clothes and come help me skin and gut the rabbit," Frank said to Jake. Jake quickly took off his outer clothes and slipped into his oversized boots and coveralls. Soon Holly and Emily were busy in the kitchen. Holly had gone to the cellar to get an onion wrapped in muslin, cool and dry in its box of sawdust shavings. She found a few carrots and brought them up as well. She replaced the trap door and saw that Emily had taken the big cast iron pot from the wall.

"How does your father like his rabbit prepared?" Holly asked.

"We make it like fried chicken," said Emily.

They poured a quantity of bacon fat into the deep pan, set aside a pie tin with a good quantity of flour for dredging and awaited the rabbit's return.

Jake came in with a longer, scrawnier pink carcass that in no way resembled the same animal that had gone outside. Jake proudly handed his day's work to Holly who laid it on the cutting board and chopped it into sections. Emily dredged it in flour and soon the cabin was smelling of hot oil and spatters.

Frank came back in and went right over to his chair and shoved a few things into his personal trunk. Holly was just about ready to tell the men to wash up when they came over and did just that. Emily left Holly to finish frying the last few pieces while she set the table. Holly took out the last few pieces with a slotted spoon and the oval platter was heaped with fried rabbit. She brought the dish to the table where everyone was seated. Holly took her seat and was prepared to say grace when Jake began instead, "Thank you Lord for this bounty. Thank you for the food you provide us and thank you for bringing us a mother who can cook biscuits and now rabbit."

Holly looked at him with wide surprised eyes. Jake gave her a smile and grabbed a big broad piece of rabbit and a biscuit. Holly figured she was blushing but she was so proud and surprised at the moment that she didn't actually care. She looked over at Frank who nodded to her and said, "Well, eat it up. Rabbit tastes best when it's hot."

Holly took a nibble from her narrow long piece and indeed it did taste like chicken. She noticed Frank watching when she took a larger bite and her face got all screwed up as she realized that mixed in with the sweet tender meat there were tiny bones. She worked one to the front of her mouth and slipped it out only to find the next time she chewed, she found two or three more. She had never worked so hard for anything she'd ever eaten. By the time she had swallowed that bite she had fished four little bones, the size of toothpicks, out of her mouth. She looked up again. Frank's face looked fit to burst. Then he let out a great laugh and the children joined in.

"You've never had fried rabbit, have you?" Frank said.

"No, I don't believe I've had the pleasure." Holly said.

"There is nothing so tasty as rabbit and nothing so darned hard to eat," Frank said. "There is no trick to it. If you don't get a flat broad piece, there is nothing for it but to pick it apart on the plate with your fingers. Try to get as many little bones out before you take a bite of it."

"So now you tell me!" Holly said with mock indignation.

"I had to watch you work it out for yourself. You were a sight. Trying to eat like a lady with a mouth full of little bones. It just can't be done. Rabbit is the most indelicate delicacy man was ever given to eat. Everyone spends more time with their fingers in the meat than putting meat into their stomach."

After that explanation, and the long laugh that followed, Holly warmed up to the task of eating rabbit. It was delicious meat but each morsel was a little battle, hard won. There was no dignified way to eat fried rabbit. Even so, it was the most enjoyable dinner Holly had ever eaten. Jake was so proud that he had bagged game for their dinner. Emily and Frank claimed it was the best fried rabbit ever.

Once dinner was cleared away and the dishes were done, Holly suggested that they begin stringing popcorn for the Christmas tree. While the popcorn was cooking, Jake gathered up colored paper, mostly from an old Sears catalogue, and tore those pages into thin long strips. Emily worked a mixture of flour and water into a paste and brought that to the table. Soon the three of them were busy either gluing together strips into a paper chain or stringing popcorn. Before bedtime there were enough lengths to decorate the entire tree. Holly asked Frank how the tree stand was coming.

"Jake, you and I can finish that tomorrow. Then we'll set up the tree in the house," Frank said.

Holly saw Jake and Emily steal looks at each other and smile. Frank may have noticed that as well, for he winked at Holly. She set upon cleaning the dining table with all her energy, she had to get to that wet paste before the glue had a chance to dry on the table. Then she swept the floor to carefully remove any stray popcorn or kernels behind. All the lengths of decoration were laid upon her arm chair, patiently awaiting their purpose. The children had gone to bed. Frank was seated at his favorite chair, thumbing through a farm catalog. It was time for her to go to bed and Holly softly told Frank, "Goodnight," before she retired.

Chapter 12

The day began with a sense of urgency. This was the last day to get everything ready for Christmas. There still seemed so much to do. Holly didn't need to remind either children to get up and do their chores. Emily happily bounded out of bed and set a pot of water on the stove to boil. Jake got up and was out the door before Emily finished making Daisy's mash. Soon the door slammed again and Holly was alone in the house. She had biscuits to make for the day and she also needed to prepare an overnight dough for Christmas day.

The house was quiet and it smelled a mixture of yeast dough and flour, sap and pine. Holly wiped the flour from her hands upon her apron. She looked out the window to see if anyone was about. She could see no one.

She took off her thin leather boots, which now had been relegated to being house shoes. She put on Margaret's larger heavy boots, added a sweater and a shawl, and headed outdoors herself. She decided to take a look in the barn and see how the mare and Emily were doing.

Holly stepped into the dark stable, there was a window near the middle toward the back that let in some light. That was near Daisy's stall. It was quiet and smelled sweetly of hay mixed with the scent of leather and an earthy smell of animals. The quiet made it seem empty. Holly looked in at the stall and there was Emily trying to comfort Daisy. The mare lifted herself with effort out of the fresh straw. She stood only for a moment and then paced and circled around the stall. Emily looked up at Holly and her face was drawn and worried.

"Why is Daisy so anxious? I can't get her to stand still," said Emily.

Daisy suddenly stopped and lowered down to lay upon her side. This caused her ribs and abdomen to shift off to one side and look disproportionately larger. Her stomach was greatly bloated and the whites of her eyes showed distress. Holly rushed in to kneel beside Emily and she was conscious that she must remain calm and in control of her emotions for everyone's sake.

Holly knelt drew her hand across the mare's belly, flank and rump.

"Can you help Daisy? She has been up and down for a couple of hours," Emily said. "I'm afraid there is something wrong."

"Looks like she is close to foaling," said Holly. She made soft soothing noises, whether for Daisy or for Emily, it didn't matter. Holly's hand felt for the edges of the foal inside. Was it breech? She scooted around to see how much Daisy was dilated and then Daisy shifted and a pink tinged spill of liquid that spread upon the straw bed.

"Is she bleeding? Oh, what is wrong?" Emily began to panic.

"Why don't you go out and find your father and bring him back here. Daisy and I will be alright until you get back. Go on dear," Holly said softly as she pushed the child out of the stall.

Holly considered it might be a mare's equivalent to "water breaking." It certainly wasn't a sign of bleeding. Still, she had never witnessed a child's birth let alone the birth of a foal. She silently prayed for Frank's swift appearance and for the safe delivery of Daisy's foal. Holly comforted the mare the best she knew how. She realized that this was all in God's hands. She reminded herself to be strong.

Soon the stall door opened and Frank knelt along beside her. His presence alone comforted her and gave her courage. He made soothing noises that served to quiet all the females. Holly leaned in and saw there was what looked to be a hoof protruding from Daisy's womb. Holly looked over to Frank. He had already moved to lend his hands to the enterprise. He rubbed Daisy's flanks firmly in short oval strokes. He then asked Holly to perform the hand rubbing for him.

Holly complied immediately, steeling her nerves. Now was not the time for hysterics. She thought of Emily's love for the horse and of all the evenings and mornings she'd dutifully fed the mare mash. Daisy was a part of the family, and Holly would do her duty to protect and aid her.

Holly stroked Daisy's flanks just as he'd asked. Frank knelt behind Daisy's flanks and helped to bring the foal along. It was a difficult task, but he also was motivated. Holly marveled at his focus and patience.

Sweat collected on Holly's brow. Her shoulders felt tense, but she ignored the ache. She, too, would come through. Silently, she prayed for Daisy's strength and health, and for the health of her foal.

Slowly, a little foal slipped out of Daisy and onto the straw, helped along by Frank. Daisy's eyes softened and became wholly brown again. With her front feet propped on the straw, her upper body arched in effort to lick the newborn foal. The foal itself had only enough energy to raise its head. It's sticky wet coat looked like it was made with matted feathers.

Emily came around and knelt between Holly and her father. Her eyes were wide with wonder, and her face shone with happiness.

Emily smiled at Holly, "Thank you. I was so afraid I would lose her."

Holly brushed her hand over the top of Emily's head and absently pulled back a hank of hair that covered her eyes. Then she gave Emily's shoulder a squeeze.

The three of them sat for a moment, captivated by the sight of Daisy licking her newborn. The newborn foal struggled to stand and nurse because his feet were awkward and overly long.

Emily gave a soft laugh that expressed her relief and happiness. Holly laughed as well and looked over at Frank who had been watching both of them.

Blushing, Holly took note of how messy she had become. All of them were damp, dirty and straw stuck to their clothes.

"Come on, let's wash up. There is more to this day than a simple foaling." Frank said.

Emily, however, did not want to go. "I'll stay just a little longer. I can't bear to leave them."

Frank held the stall door open for Holly and he led her through the darkened barn. Once outside, he motioned for her to follow him around the backside of the barn towards the pig yards.

Jake dug his pitchfork into scraps and tossed them across the yard. He wore old coveralls of a heavy broadcloth and shoes much too large for his feet. Hungry pigs came towards him. The biggest ones were in front. Smaller ones tried to squeeze in between the spaces. Jake tried to throw scraps over their heads to give the smaller ones a chance. He tried to stay out of their yard but sometimes he had to step into the pen with them. This feeding was a distraction, so that they would pay attention to food and leave him alone.

Frank had two hammers in his hand and carried a board. He called to Jake, "I need your help replacing that rail." Jake cut through the pig pen at the center and leaned his pitchfork against the post. By the time Holly had caught up to them, they were both hammering on the rail, Jake from the inside the pen and Frank from the outside.

Her eyes marveled, shuttling back and forth, between the man and the boy who was a postage stamp sized image of the same coin. Frank looked up and caught her smiling.

Holly was taken by surprise at being unexpectedly seen. "I have been here just under a week and so far, and I'm not really sure there is such a thing as an ordinary day at the Motherwell farm," she called out in a good natured voice.

"As far as today and this foaling, no, to tell the truth, this has never happened before," Frank replied.

Jake's eyes suddenly lit up. He squirmed and held himself back long enough to say, "Daisy had her foal? Can I go see now?"

"Yes son, you run along now. It is still brand new to this world. Go and see it. Maybe you can give Emily a hand as well."

Jake may have missed hearing the last phrase. He leaped like a frog. One moment he was bent over in the mud and the next he was flinging himself over the rail. The sudden separation of his huge shoes coming out of the heavy sludge made a loud suction sound. He was so eager he nearly ran out of his oversized mud covered boots. His frantic effort to run in two sets of overalls made a sound like wet sails in the wind. No excess of outerwear could restrain him.

Holly watched his comical figure retreat and enter the barn. She realized now she and Frank were alone.

"You have a wonderful family, Frank."

"I'm glad to hear you say that. I've wanted them to have a woman's influence. Growing up without a mother is difficult. Now you are here, they don't need to suffer."

"What are you saying? No one should have to suffer," Holly turned toward him with a frown.

"After a while, it becomes a habit, I suppose," said Frank

"I know all about habits," said Holly. "Remember, I grew up in an orphanage and was raised by Sister Maybelle."

"I guess you do. I just meant to say that with you coming to us, they won't have to suffer. I just wonder whether this arrangement suits you too," said Frank. He ran his hand through his hair and blew out air threw his nose. He looked for all the world like an animal himself, testing the air to see whether to run or to stand.

"I told you at the station that I was used to hard work. You can trust me to keep my word. Your letter gave me a choice. I could stay and be a burden at the orphanage or I could chose to make a difference in your family's life. I volunteered to come here, and you asked. It was my choice. I don't see this new life as cause for suffering," said Holly.

"I know Holly. We made this bargain before you knew anything about us. I was just wondering if you had any change of heart since coming here," Frank had both hands firmly on the rail and his eyes stared ahead. They didn't seem focused on anything in particular.

"We made a bargain. I keep my word. I wasn't promised love and you weren't promised anything but a mother for your children," said Holly.

She took a step away from Frank, surprised at her speech, a little out of breath. What had brought that on? Was it the strangeness of her life proving to be so much what she'd wanted in her deepest heart? Was it that she was now in such proximity to this kind and quiet man? In the barn, he had seemed so sure of himself, his hands were strong and deft.

This was the first time they had spoken to each other directly about their 'arrangement'. Why had she been so adamant? She hadn't expected to care so soon. Her heart ached for the children and she was becoming mesmerized by this tall lean man named Frank. Suddenly, she realized that she wanted more than just the duties of a mother for his children. She wanted to be needed and necessary in their lives.

Patience, it all takes patience. Patience, however, wasn't her strong suit.

"I need to get back to the house and check on the biscuits," said Holly. It took all her strength to walk back to the house. She dared not look back or talk to Frank any further. She feared that all the good things she was trying to do would work against her somehow.

What would Sister Maybelle say? Well, that was easy to figure out. Sister Maybelle would tell her to stop, because none of this was about her. She needed to support, not to take.

But standing on the sidelines was difficult when Holly had grown so attached to the children and to Frank. Being an orphan herself, these motherless children tugged at her heartstrings. All her life, she had longed for stability, a family to call her own, and a home. She had always dreamed that there was a place where she belonged, with people who weren't interchangeable. People whom she could call her own.

Holly focused on her soup until it began to boil. Then, she moved the pot to the front edge of the stove and reached inside the door and banked the wood all to the backside. Now the soup could simmer and be left alone. But what was she to do?

A quick glance around Frank's home showed her everything was clean and in its place. They had all accomplished so much since she first arrived and everything was covered in dust. The house had always been solid and warm, but now it was clean and inviting. The tree was decorated by their own hands and stationed in the stand that Frank and Jake had built. Homemade presents lied beneath it, wrapped in colorful scraps of fabric and tied with twine.

Holly doubted her heart had ever felt so full. She brought her hand to her chest, inhaling deeply the scent of fresh pine and simmering soup. She was positively simmering herself. No, she was brimming over with gratitude and happiness.

Frank had given her so much. Why did she have to push him about church?

Holly glanced out the windows. Frank and the children were still doing their part. She wanted to continue to do her part, too.

Holly decided to go check on Jake and Emily. When she entered the barn, she saw that all the old straw had been removed and replaced so the new mamma and her foal had a clean spot. Daisy had licked him down and his coat was dry and fluffy. They both had clean blankets cinched to their backs. The foal nursed and Emily sat in the corner of the stall on a bale of hay with a dreamy peaceful face. Jake leaned against the stall with his face pressed between the slats.

Jake had apparently carted the old straw away and fed it to the pigs, much to their delight. Emily was quietly keeping watch, both delighting in the new life and seeking to protect and nurture it. In the coming days there would be many extra chores for both children but from the looks on their faces, they were glad of the opportunity.

Emily glanced up at Holly. "I didn't see you come in," she said.

Holly smiled. "You were busy."

Emily wiped her eyes. "I still have work to do."

Holly raised her brows.

"Holly," she began slowly, "Will you come with me back into the house? There is something I'd like to do together."

Holly nodded, following the young girl back to the house. Once inside, Emily excused herself to her room, and then came back with her knitting. "How do I finish this hat?" she asked.

Holly couldn't have been happier to show her. "Come, sit with me. I'll get my knitting out and together we will finish both hats."

They sat together on the faded rose settee and Holly showed Emily how to cast off the stitches, one by one, until the hat was released from the knitting needles and stood on its own.

"Now you tie a knot at the last stitch and with a darning needle, you feed the loose thread back into the body of the hat. There. That looks perfect."

Emily looked up to Holly and her face beamed with pride.

"Just look at that beautiful hat. Your father will appreciate it even more because it was made by your hands," Holly said.

"I could never have done it without you. Thank you, uh, Holly."

"Do you want to practice some more? I still haven't cast off Jake's hat. Here, you work on mine and I will go find something we can wrap these up."

Holly left Emily bent over her work, giving her opportunity to repeat the lesson that she had just learned, but this time without reminders or prompts. Holly felt sure that Emily had mastered the process. She went to the closet and picked out two bandanas and some twine. However, when she returned, Emily was no longer working.

Holly crouched next to the girl. Holly saw that Emily's eyes were glassy and, for a moment, her heart stopped. "What's wrong Emily?"

Emily was silent for a few moments. Finally, in a soft voice she choked out, "I'm sorry."

Holly placed a hand on the girl's shoulder. She didn't need to ask what Emily was sorry about. She already knew.

"I told you that I've already forgiven you," Holly whispered.

Emily cringed. "That just makes it worse."

"No, it doesn't," Holly said. "It only means that you must forgive yourself."

"You're so nice to me," she whimpered. "I was so mean, and you're still so nice. Why?"

Holly rubbed Emily's back. "You're young, Emily. And, more than that, you've been through more than any little girl should go through."

"So did you. You didn't even have your mom," Emily cried. "And what I said was a lie. She would have loved you. She should have loved you."

"Everyone makes mistakes," Holly said. "You should learn from your mistakes, but not let them govern your actions. Use them to become more compassionate, not to revel in your guilt."

Emily sniffled, rubbing her eyes. "But aren't you mad at me for the things I said?"

"I do not delight in anger, but in mercy," Holly told the girl, paraphrasing a quote from *Micah*.

And then, Emily did something that Holly never would have expected. In fact, something that Holly never would have even dreamed could happen.

She hugged her.

Emily's little arms wrapped around Holly's body, and Holly felt as if she were being surrounded by light and beauty. Old pains that had long since been buried resurfaced. The sorrow of being alone after being abandoned by her mother. Of watching other children walk down the street, hand in hand with their mothers. Holly's heart had known envy, then. And, because she had been envious, that same heart had known guilt, for how could Holly wish those happy little girls any ill will? To do so would be to take pleasure in another's suffering, which Holly could never do.

Still, she had thought those horrible thoughts. Though she'd prayed alongside Sister Maybelle for years for the salvation of those who had strayed from the path, she'd never prayed for herself. A part of her had always thought she wasn't worth it. Sometimes, the hardest and most important thing to do was to forgive yourself.

"Forgive yourself," Holly whispered, holding Emily tighter. But the words were for Emily as much as they were for herself. The two of them hugged one another, delighting in mercy, delighting in forgiveness, delighting in new love.

"Thank you," Emily whispered into Holly's shoulder. "Thank you for being my mother. I'm so happy you are here, and I'm sorry if I ever made anything difficult for you."

Holly smiled as tears ran down her face. "You do not make anything difficult, little one. You make everything worthwhile."

Slowly, Holly pulled away. Tenderly, she wiped the tears from under Emily's eyes. "Now, let's get these gifts ready," she said.

Emily nodded enthusiastically, giving her a short nervous laugh. Then, they got to work. By the time Jake and Frank had come back into the house two more presents were tucked beneath the tree.

Chapter 13

Holly woke with her heart pounding with excitement. It was Christmas day. Dawn had broken and Holly could make out the sky turning from slate to a paler shade of grey. Free of clouds and crisp as starched linen, the day promised to spread out wide like a starched sheet.

Quickly, she got out of bed and dressed. Her breath came out in gusts of vapor. How cold it had turned overnight! Hopefully the newborn foal and his recovering mother were warm. She hastened to pull on her woolen socks and Margaret's boots beneath her petticoat and long broadcloth skirt. Then, she splashed a bit of water on her face, pulled a brush through her hair, and drew a shawl over her blouse. It was time to start a fire in the stove.

As soon as she entered the main room, the smell of pine and sap and popcorn met her nose. Smiling, she looked over at the noble fir tree standing upright and stiff in its stand. Since the sun was below the western ridge, the morning light was diffuse. Soon enough, the children would wake, do their chores, want breakfast, and then gather round the Christmas tree to see what those presents contained.

She was just as full of anticipation as the children. Not for what was under the tree, for she was certain that she knew the inventory. No, she was eager to see their faces and experience Christmas once again through their young eyes. Today was her chance to make a difference in these children's lives. Holly might not have received much of a formal education, but she did know the true meaning of Christmas. It was something she intended to share with her new family, for everyone deep down needed and deserved love.

Holly began with breakfast. She went to the shelf and lifted the muslin cloth from the bowl. The sourdough had doubled in size overnight. The sponge was exactly like its name, little bubbles of dough dimpled over its contour like the surface of the moon. *Perfect.*

She reached for a shaker of cinnamon sugar and another shaker of flour. She turned out the sponge and breathed in its yeasty fragrance. She kneaded the dough into the floured board, pressed it down in a rough circle, and coated it with cinnamon sugar.

Rolling it up and folding in the ends, she began kneading it again. She pressed it into a flat disc and poured on the spicy sugar until it threatened to spill over. Her arms began to feel warm and tired, but now was not the time to rest. Instead, she manipulated the dough into a long roll and then took a knife and cut it into two inch discs. They looked like spirals. Finally, she arranged the rolls on a wide iron sheet, covered them with muslin cloth and left them to rise on the warming shelf.

Emily was the first to wake. She came into the kitchen and sniffed the air. A wide smile spread over her lips and she dashed over to Holly to peek at what was beneath the muslin cloth.

"Don't touch, you'll disturb the rise," Holly said. "I've got some water on the boil for Daisy's hot mash."

"That's right. It's Christmas and Daisy has a foal. Oh Holly, this is the most exciting day. I can't wait to see Jake's and father's face when they open their presents."

"And we need to celebrate Christmas. Our morning is so full. I hope we aren't rushing through it," murmured Holly.

"No, I can't wait to celebrate the whole day. But first I'll feed Daisy and look in on the foal. I've decided to name him Winter."

"Very good. Here is the hot mash."

Holly watched Emily carry the small bucket outside. Snow blanketed the ground, so the little girl had to navigate through a few inches of white in order to get to the barn. The snow was why everything was so diffuse and bright even though the sun hadn't actually risen.

"It's beautiful," Holly whispered.

"What did you say?" Jake asked, walking into the kitchen.

"It has snowed," Holly said, turning.

"It snowed?" The boy yelled excitedly. "On Christmas day?" His smile was so wide that his adult upper teeth showed their serrated edges. Racing to the coat rack, Jake grabbed his coat and his father's hat. He shoved his feet into the oversized boots.

"Be careful!" Holly called out as Jake ripped open the door, letting in a gust of cold wind.

He looked back and gave Holly a bright smile over his shoulder. "I will!"

Seconds later, the door closed and she was alone.

Holly walked to the window and scanned the farm for a sight of Frank. She wondered how early he had risen and what he was doing. She watched Jake lumber over to the pig sty, with his oversized boots taking steps that seemed impossibly spaced. He even walked like Frank she realized with a smile and her breath gave a little hitch. She swallowed hard and rubbed her hands briskly on her apron.

Holly checked on the rolls. They had nearly doubled in size. She opened the oven and spread the coals out evenly with a poker and then placed the iron sheet above the coals on a metal riser that kept them from actually touching the embers. She shut the door and told herself to remove them in thirty minutes. One always knew they were ready by the smell of cinnamon and sugar and wonderful bread wafting in the air.

Holly went outside to check the chicken coop. She opened the door and ducked down inside. Her hands searched out each and every nest. The hens seemed to cluck *tisk, tisk* as she disturbed their winter naps.

There were fewer eggs today than last week. She saw evidence of feathers on the straw nests, and even more upon the floor. They were molting and the eggs would be fewer and fewer for the next month or so. This was the time for them to rest and gather their strength. They deserved it for giving so much. More than that, they needed it. They looked a sorry lot right now, shabby with patches of worn feathers covering them.

However, it wouldn't be like this for them too much longer. In a few months they would return to their usual yield, looking dignified and lush with bright feathers. Holly was happy the hens hadn't completely stopped laying yet.

"Thank you, dears! You have made our Christmas breakfast one of joy and delight. Sorry to disturb, go back to your naps." Holly was in such a good mood she didn't even worry about conversing with chickens. As she crossed the yard with her bounty, she spied Frank attaching the harness to the wagon. The leather positively glowed from being freshly cleaned and oiled.

"Looking mighty supple," she said with a bright voice.

"You don't look so bad yourself this fine morning," Frank said.

"Oh, I was talking about the leather harness. It seems transformed." Immediately, Holly turned pink and stammered. Why had she spoken to him like that?

"Today of all days, Buck wants to look his best," Frank told her.

Holly couldn't help but frown. Why would that matter? Was it because Frank was finally being touched by the Christmas spirit?

She decided to play along. Frank's goodwill and pride deserved to be acknowledged and supported. "Is he going somewhere?" Holly asked.

Frank looked down, smiling slowly. "Maybe. That depends on you."

Now Holly was very confused. "What do you mean?"

Frank patted Buck's back. "You'll see," he said. "It isn't time yet."

"It isn't time yet for what?" Holly couldn't help but ask.

"You'll see," Frank said, giving her another cryptic smile.

Holly felt her face begin to flush. Suddenly, it didn't seem so cold outside. "Well, breakfast will be ready soon," she said. "After that, we're opening presents."

"I'll be right in," Frank called after her.

She was nearly to the front porch when she felt a sudden nudge on her shoulder accompanied by a soft *thwack*. Her neck grew cold with the edges of little snowflakes. *No.*

She turned upon her heel to face the attacker. What she found was Frank's plain, wide eyed, smiling face.

"You?" she asked.

Frank's smile grew even wider.

Emily and Jake returned, done with their chores. Silently, they looked from their father to her and back to their father. Without a word Jake dove for the snow and scooped up a double handful that he clapped quickly into a snowball. Then, he launched it hitting his father squarely in the jaw.

Had Jake just defended her?

Seconds later Emily followed suit,
only *her* snowball was launched at Holly. However,
Holly was ready. She ducked, narrowly missing the
lob. Still, the quick motion had taken its toll on Holly.
Both feet slipped out from under her as she lost her
balance.

Holly flailed her arms, trying to regain her
balance, but it was too late. She was going down.
Then, all of a sudden, she stopped falling. Something
had stopped her.

Large hands caught her descending form in a firm
grip. Holly looked up to find Frank's sturdy shoulders
standing over her. Swiftly, he hoisted her up just as
her backside was about to land in the snow.

Holly dangled there for a moment while the
children held their breath and then burst out in
laughter. Though her heart was still beating furiously,
the humor of the situation hadn't eluded her. How
silly she must look! Laughter bubbled up inside her.
She glanced up at Frank.

Her laughter stopped cold. Her smile froze.

His eyes were filled with concern. He gave a quick
jerk upward and she cascaded into his chest. Was that
his heart beating so quickly and fast? She didn't have

time to test her theory, for he immediately pulled away and set her back down on her feet.

"I think we got a little carried away," he murmured into her ear. His warm breath made her neck tingle. As did his smell, a mix of leather and musk.

Holly was glad her face was turned, for she feared her cheeks were bright red!

She stepped back. "Come on, children!" she said. "Let's go inside for breakfast and see what is under that Christmas tree."

That was all it took to shift the children's attention from the fact that Holly had momentarily been in Frank's arms.

She fidgeted with the hem of her cloak while everyone filed through the door. Unfortunately, merely mentioning Christmas and presents wasn't enough to distract her from Frank's strong embrace. In fact, she feared nothing would.

Still, Holly couldn't afford to be distracted. If this was to be the perfect Christmas she wanted it to be, she had to focus on her role as hostess. Frank pulled away from her, following the children. The sudden absence of his touch made her feel unsteady. She looked down at her basket and saw with relief that not one of the eggs she had gathered had broken. She went back inside, putting the cold and the memory of Frank behind her.

Chapter 14

"The house smells wonderful!" Emily said as she took off her coat.

"I can't wait to eat and open presents," Jake cried as he kicked off his boots.

"Must not disappoint the children," Frank leaned over Holly's shoulder. For some odd reason she could not ignore him when he was so close by.

Holly hurried to the kitchen and cracked the eggs into a skillet. Emily set the table and Frank and Jake washed their hands. When the eggs were done, Holly pulled out the hot pinwheels from the stove and put them on a platter along with a pot of butter on to the table. There was a sprig of Holly and a tip from the fir tree's branch in a medicine bottle on the table. Had Emily added that touch of decoration for their table? Holly took a quick breath and began, "We honor this day of Your birth with gifts of our own to each other, with food that is served with love and with gratitude that You have given us so many blessings. Amen."

Holly watched with pleasure as she saw everyone dig in to the sourdough sweet rolls.

"This is a breakfast feast," Frank said.

"I love these rolls. Even the eggs taste better today!" exclaimed Jake.

"Thank you for the pretty bouquet, Emily. It really shows this is a special occasion," said Holly.

"I didn't put that on the table," said Emily who gave her father a hard direct look.

"It was me. I thought the table needed a piece of the tree. And I found a sprig of holly. I thought that was important. So much has changed now you've come to us," Frank said with his head down, which made his eyes seem to peer out at her from beneath his brow.

"I love this sweet bread but I want to open my presents," Jake said in a pleading voice.

"Go ahead, you can take your roll to the tree and open up your present," Holly said.

Immediately the children scooted out from the table and each grabbed a roll and ran over to squat at the tree. Jake handed Emily a lump of fabric. Emily handed her father two presents. Holly handed Jake his present. Frank went over to his chair and reached into his reading basket and pulled out a bundle for

Holly. When they were all seated around the tree, each of them began to open their presents.

Emily exclaimed at her darning form, "Jake, this is just what I needed. Look Holly! Won't this work well?"

Holly smiled at both of them. "Jake, that is as fine a darning form as I have ever seen. Yes, that is just the tool that is needed."

Jake opened up his present and immediately put the knitted hat on his head. "Now I'll not have to wear my father's big hat. This one is so much warmer and it fits perfectly!" He gave everyone a smile. "I love it Holly. Thank you so much."

"There is one more for you, Jake," said Holly. She handed Jake a small parcel which he quickly unwound. There was his little mug with a hairline crack down the side and on its handle was a red grosgrain ribbon loop. Jake held it tenderly and then smiled at Holly.

"It's now an ornament for the tree. In honor of your mother. Why don't you choose where to hang it?" Holly suggested.

Jake went right over and stepped up onto the arm of the settee and looped the mug as high as his arm could reach.

Emily walked over and dropped the biggest bundle wrapped in sheeting onto her father's lap. Frank quickly opened it and out spilled all of his wool socks. He held one up and inspected the heel and the toe and said, "Emily! These all are as good as new. Now my toes won't be cold or chaffed by the boot. I have as many socks as any rich man. Thank you."

Emily beamed and gave Holly a private little wink.

Next, Frank opened his other present and saw his new knitted hat. "Emily, you can knit?"

"Yes," Emily said. "Holly taught me."

Frank was astounded. "What wonders you have learned. I will wear your hat every day!"

"You don't have to wear it when it's hot out," Emily piped up.

"Holly. You haven't opened up your present," Jake said.

"It's your turn," Emily said.

Holly unwrapped her bundle and the most luxurious soft white fur fell in her lap. It was the pelt from the snowshoe rabbit. "Oh, this is the most beautiful thing I have ever received. It is gloriously soft and supple," Holly exclaimed.

"It is a muff!, And it's from all of us," Emily cried out.

"I shot the rabbit and father tanned it," Jake said.

"I fashioned it into a muff," said Emily. "At first I was going to make it into a hat and use my head as a model."

"That would have been alright since I have a small head," laughed Holly.

"But there wasn't time. I've noticed that your hands get cold so I made it into a muff and I used the whole pelt," said Emily.

Holly slipped her hands into the muff. "It feels divine. I can't decide whether I want my hands to be warm or whether I just want to touch the softness outside. I love it. Thank you, all of you. This is the sweetest Christmas present I've ever received," Holly blinked and smiled at every one.

Emily beamed, looking so youthful and so beautiful. Holly remembered with a surprise that her first impression of Emily was that the girl seemed older than her age. Her rigid expression was replaced with animation. She was no longer afraid to show joy and hold back her laughter.

Holly then regarded at Jake. He also wore a smile, albeit a toothy one, as he marveled at the red wool knitted hat atop his head that so perfectly complimented his freckles.

Lastly, she looked to Frank. His face was flushed with warmth that seemed to embrace and infect everyone around him. She had found him stiff and cold when she had first met him. When had he become the warm hub of this happy family?

Frank met Holly's gaze. "There's one last present," he said, "though you won't find it under the tree."

Holly was speechless. What did he mean? She looked to the children, but they seemed just as stupefied as she was.

"Frank?" she asked. "I don't understand, where would it be?"

His grin deepened, and although she felt uncertain, something about the kind look in his eyes made her heart feel at ease. She trusted Frank. She had faith in him.

"Come on everyone!" he said. "Back outside!"

The children leaped up. Excitement buzzed around the small room as though all of a sudden everyone realized that anything was possible. It was Christmas day and there was one more present. Holly couldn't help but get caught up in the mystery of it.

Frank came over and offered Holly his hand. "Come on, Holly," he said. "It's your present. If you don't come outside with us, then all of my work is for naught."

Holly accepted his hand and allowed Frank to pull her to her feet. Those happy, floaty feelings she'd felt earlier during the snowfight returned. He was so close, but this time he wasn't pushing her away. She felt like he was pulling her closer...into his heart.

Frank let go of Holly only to hand her her cloak. Then, he knelt and placed Margaret's boots on her feet. Holly had never been the recipient of such royal treatment, and she didn't know what to do with herself.

The children knew, however. They danced around them, telling them to hurry up. They wanted to know what the surprise was waiting outside even more than Holly did. "Alright, alright!" she laughed as the children ushered her outside. To them, she couldn't get out the door fast enough.

Holly stumbled on the porch. When she looked out into the yard, her breath caught in her throat.

There was Buck. A wreath of evergreen was on his bridle. Two more wreaths decorated the sides of the cart, each tied with a bright red ribbon. As if aware of all the admiration he was receiving, Buck lowered his head and raised one front hoof, creating a picture reminiscent of a Christmas steed pulling a sleigh.

"Oh my," Holly said, bringing her hand to her chest. "When did you do all this?"

"While you were making breakfast," Frank said. Then, he stepped forward off the porch. When his boots reached the snow, he turned and raised his hand to Holly, silently asking her to take it.

She stood still, unable to process what was happening.

"Come on, Holly," he said. "Haven't we got somewhere to go? What do you say?"

"Where are we going?" Holly asked.

He gave her a handsome, comforting smile. "Wherever you want."

Holly's heart began to ache. Did this mean? No, he couldn't possibly. Frank Motherwell tolerated her faith, but he himself wanted nothing to do with the church.

"Where do you want to go, Holly?" he asked.

"Yeah, where are we going?" Emily piped in.

"I want to know too!" Jake exclaimed.

Holly opened her eyes. Though it was cold, she had to blink several times to keep them dry. "Frank, don't ask me this," she begged.

"Why?" he asked.

"Because, you told me not to mention it...You told me..."

"It doesn't matter what I said before," Frank reassured her. "This is my true Christmas gift to you. I want to take you where you want to go. *Anywhere* you want to go."

Holly shut her eyes and hugged her chest. Was he truly giving her license to say it? "Church," she whispered. "I want to go to church."

She waited for the reprimand. For the cold shoulder. For the regret. It did not come. When she opened her eyes, Frank was smiling at her just as he had before. No, actually his smile was even sweeter than it had been. There was a new softness in his eyes.

"Church?" Jake asked. "I thought she was going to say the candy store."

Frank laughed. "This is Holly's Christmas present, not yours. Come on, everyone! Get into the cart. We're going to church!"

Chapter 15

The sun was just coming up over the ridge as Frank snapped the reins and sent Buck on his way toward town. They were all bundled together under a coverlet. Emily nestled between Holly and Frank while Jake sat on her lap.

Holly grabbed Emily's near hand and pulled it into the muff along with hers. Then Holly gave Emily's hand a squeeze. Holly readjusted the coverlet and rearranged her arms to hold Jake comfortably. Even though he was a bit heavy, and a bit worried that her legs would go numb under his weight, Holly wouldn't have it any other way. The world felt warm and hospitable, even in the midst of a snow covered landscape. It felt that way not only because they were bundled up and warm, but because they were a *family*.

Holly looked over at Frank. What did he think about this jam of bodies all riding on the bench together? She couldn't tell, for her husband just stared straight ahead. Clicking his tongue, he kept Buck going at a steady brisk pace. He was focused on getting them to their destination on time.

When they arrived at church the lot was nearly full with other wagons and carriages. Most were drawn with horses, but some with mules and oxen. Others came on foot. It didn't matter how they had arrived, or whether it was in a humble or a grand manner. The important thing was that they were here.

Everyone was in their best and cleanest clothes to show their respect and concern for each other. They came to worship God, and their hearts bent upon gratitude and prayer for the birth of His son, their Savior.

At the entrance, men tipped their hats and women nodded and spoke warm greetings. Even Frank greeted the man who stood at the entrance. "Good morning, deacon Jackson."

The deacon returned Frank's hello with the same friendly nod he gave everyone. As soon as they entered, it was obvious that the church was nearly full. Still, Frank was able to find a pew with space enough for them all. He stood aside as Jake then Emily then Holly filed in. Frank himself took the seat next to the aisle.

Holly breathed in deeply. The air was lightly scented with beeswax, sap, and evergreens. The hymnals were numbered on the dark weathered wood walls. The altar was simply decorated with candles set among pine and fir boughs that encircled a pine cradle. Stationed above the raised pulpit, the wooden cross was also framed by fir boughs.

Although Holly missed the familiarity of her old church in Manchester, this small plain church suited her tastes more closely. She imagined these people had grown up here, had known each other their whole lives and she felt a touch of jealousy and awe. Then she caught herself and smiled. Now she had the opportunity to be one of them, a member of this town. She realized there was another level of family she hadn't considered, that of belonging to a community.

The chatter soon quieted to murmurs. A few coughed. Some people shuffled to get comfortably seated.

Holly did not have to wait long for pastor Smith's arrival. He came forward and raised his arms for all to stand and said, "I invite you all to stand and pray along with me."

Pastor Smith was old and his voice was was mellow but not strong. Those at the back strained to hear some of what he said to the congregation. He was a good Christian man and, especially on this auspicious day, Holly was disposed to think well of all things with her family alongside her.

Her heart swelled as they were asked to sing a hymn she regarded as an old friend, "The First Noel."

Holly smiled as she heard Emily's voice once again. Cautiously so Emily would not see, Holly nudged Frank. When she caught his attention, she tilted her head over to indicate Emily. Holly lifted her eyes and pressed her hands together and he seemed to understand what she meant. He gave her the warmest smile.

Holly remembered their almost embrace. Her voice wavered but she managed to keep singing. When the song was finished they sat back in the pew.

Holly turned to Emily and whispered to her, "I love hearing you sing. You have the voice of an angel."

"Really?" Emily whispered.

Holly nodded, for Pastor Smith was about to speak, and she had no intention of disturbing the service. Then, they all stood again for a reading of Psalm 45.

She looked over to the dear downturned heads of Emily and Jake. She was pleased to see Jake frown as he focused on reading the lines precisely. Emily also took it seriously, running her finger under the small lines as she read aloud. As Holly spoke the familiar lines with her new family and new community, her heart began to soar.

They sat again. Pastor Smith stood on the pulpit. This time, everyone was on the edge of their pews. Before, his voice might have seemed soft, but now it was filled with new strength.

"Today we celebrate the birth of our Savior, Jesus Christ. His birth sent a message to all generations for ever more. The message of loving one another, the gift of knowing God's love for us was so great that he sent his only son. In St. John, iv.7, *Beloved, let us love one another; for love is of God; and every one that loves is born of God and knows God. He that loves not does not know God; for God is love.*"

Holly felt something touch her hand. She looked down to see Frank's fingers intertwined with hers.

When she looked up at his face, he was focused entirely on Pastor Smith.

"God is love," Pastor Smith continued. "*He who dwells in love dwells with God, and God with him. Here on earth, our love is made perfect. There is no fear in love, for perfect love casts out fear.*"

Holly squeezed Frank's hand, and he squeezed hers back. Her eyes began to water as she realized what was happening. Frank was allowing love back into his heart.

Pastor Smith's clear voice seemed to celebrate this development. "As we celebrate this day, I ask you to celebrate your love for one another. God's love for you is unconditional and perfect. Use His love as an example for us to try to love each other and ourselves more purely. Amen."

The sermon was over. The organist began to play a few chords and Holly's heart leaped. "O Holy Night". She leaned her head closer to hear Emily sing the words of this hymn. Together, they followed the score and the words and by the second verse Emily's voice grew in confidence and Holly felt no angel in heaven could have sung this song more beautifully.

She gave Emily's shoulders a squeeze when the song was done.

People filed out of the church. Many gave the family a close look and tried to catch their eye. They nodded to Holly and then to Frank. Some greeted him by name. Holly wondered why Frank hadn't stood up and led them out of the church. But he seemed determined to stay.

Finally, he turned to Emily and Jake and said, "You children go on outside. I have something I wish to say to your mother."

Emily and Jake looked at each other. Emily giggled, "Come on. Let's go get cookies next door at the pastor's house."

"Cookies?" Jake's ears perked up.

Emily rolled her eyes. "Were you not listening? They are giving children cookies next door!"

"Yes, let's go!" Jake agreed, taking his sister's hand.

Holly watched them go but did not follow. Frank's hand gripped hers tightly, and she knew she needed to hear whatever it was he wanted to say.

Finally, the last few people filed out of the church, leaving them alone.

Chapter 16

Dear Lord, give me strength, Holly prayed. She knew she had nothing to fear from her husband, but she feared her poor heart could only take so much in one day. It was already more full than it ever had been, and now it was in danger of spilling over.

The pews were cramped and made sure there was little space between them. Frank's knee bumped against hers as he turned to face her.He looked searchingly into her eyes and said with a very serious voice, "Holly, I need to ask your permission to change our agreement."

Holly stiffened. Did he want to send her away? Did he bring her here to soften the blow? "No," she blurted out. "Please don't change anything. I'm very happy with our agreement. I am happy to have a home and to be mother of your children. We had a bargain."

He squeezed her hand once again. "But love cannot be bargained for."

Holly's poor heart felt as pitiful as a shattered stained glass window. Her eyes filled with tears that threatened to spill. "Please," she whispered, "I know what you are trying to do, and I cannot abide by it."

Frank looked crestfallen. "You can't?"

"No, I can't," Holly said. "Our agreement means so much to me. I could not stand it if things changed."

Frank's jaw tightened. He looked down. "Is that really what you want?"

"Yes!" Holly exclaimed. "And I think Jake and Emily would agree with me. At least, I hope they would. We have grown so close and been through so much these past few weeks."

"Yes, that's why this change is necessary," Frank said. "My children want what I want, I guarantee it."

Emily's broken heart shattered into a million pieces. *No.* Emily and Jake too? Emily had called her mother just the other night, and Jake had protected her during the snowball fight. She had to mean something to them, didn't she? They meant so much to her.

No, they meant everything.

Holly closed her eyes and bit her lower lip, struggling not to sob. Tears now flowed freely down her cheeks. She knew that God never gave anyone more trials than they could handle, but she didn't know if she could survive this. She'd come so far and gotten so close. To have it all pulled out from under her, and on Christmas, the very day love and forgiveness and family were celebrated, was too much.

She could not bring herself to look at his face, so she stared at the hymn board instead. The numbers were bleary and out of focus.

"Please," she whispered. "Please, Frank. Do not send me away."

"Send you away?" Frank yelled.

Was that surprise in his voice? Holly looked over to see Frank's face twisted with confusion.

Did she dare to hope? Could her heart handle it? *Yes*, she decided. Yes, it could handle anything for love and family.

"You don't want to send me away?" Holly guessed.

"Of course not!" Frank declared. "I want you to be my wife."

Holly's mouth fell open. "What?"

Frank ran his free hand through his hair. "This isn't going the way I expected. Let me try again," he said.

Holly sat silently, not daring to speak.

Frank took a deep breath. "I need to tell you how I feel. After Margaret died, I vowed never to love another woman. However, I did this for myself. I know she would have wanted me to love again. She was not the kind of person who wanted anyone to close off their heart. In fact, she was very much like you in that way. Perhaps that is part of the reason why you have so thoroughly breached my defenses."

Holly's throat was so full she could barely breathe.

"I have watched how the children have taken to you. How much you have to offer them. How much you have to offer everyone. You are the kind of woman who deserves love and, most of all, the kind of woman I want to love. No, that's not it: the kind of woman I can't help but love."

He gripped her hands and brought them to his chest so she could feel his swiftly beating heart.

"I didn't want this love, Holly. I didn't want you. But now, I can't imagine living without you or living with you without loving you. I know this isn't what you signed up for, so I must ask. Holly, we are already married, but will you become my wife?"

Holly couldn't believe her ears. "Are you proposing to me?" she whispered.

"Yes. I am. I'm proposing to you in the way I should have proposed to you the first time. Unfortunately it sometimes takes me a few tries to get something right."

Holly thought that the pew beneath her had fallen away. She felt a sudden dizziness and disorientation. But a feeling deeper than either of those things took hold of her heart. Her deepest wish was coming true. Loving light cut through her confusion, leading her towards an answer and towards what she knew her true purpose in life to be.

"Yes," she said through her tears. "Yes. Yes. Yes. There is nothing I want more on this earth."

Then, Frank pulled her into his arms. "Thank you," he said as if she had just given him the best Christmas gift she could have ever given him. And perhaps she had, but he had given her something even more beautiful: A Christmas miracle.

***

Holly and Frank walked hand in hand out of the church into a bright and sunny snow-covered outdoors. Her eyes rimmed with unshed tears and her heart sang inside her chest.

Frank called out to pastor Smith, "That was a wonderful sermon we heard this morning! You may expect to see a lot of us."

Pastor Smith smiled. "That is wonderful to hear, Mr. Motherwell." He turned to Holly. "*And* Mrs. Motherwell. It was a pleasure to marry you, and I couldn't be happier to hear that we will all be seeing more of both of you."

Holly smiled. "Thank you."

She glanced at her husband to find that he was smiling too. She could see no trace of anger or resentment in his heart. He looked free.

"Is that Jake and Emily?" Frank asked as two little ones rushed towards them across the snow.

"Ah, it looks like they found my wife's cookies," Pastor Smith said.

"That doesn't surprise me," Frank muttered good naturedly.

Pastor Smith laughed as they said their goodbyes.

The children were upon them mere seconds later, cookies in one hand and a mug of hot apple cider in the other.

Emily looked back and forth from Holly to her father, "Something is different about you two," she said.

Holly blushed. Her husband, however, did not have any shred of embarrassment about telling them. "I proposed to Holly and she agreed to be my wife as well as being your mother."

"You're our real mother now?" Jake asked, his little voice rose higher and he gave Holly a shy smile.

"I am. You will still have your angel mother but I will be your mother on earth. From now until death do us part," Holly replied. She looked over to Emily whose face wore a buttoned up smile. "I am your mother too, Emily. I already love the two of you more than my heart can contain."

Emily, however, did not look upset. Instead, she exclaimed, "We got a mother on Christmas!"

Holly wasn't able to contain herself any longer. She spread out her arms and grabbed them both into an embrace, nearly spilling the hot cider. Emily dropped one cookie into the snow.

Immediately, Holly picked it up and blew off the snow, "Good as new."

"No, it is better for getting a cookie kiss from my mother," Emily said.

Frank smiled with pride. "Come on, all of you. Buck wants to get back home to his feedbag and the shelter of the barn. A farmer's family always seems to have more chores than hands to get everything done. I'll bet Daisy is looking forward to her hot mash."

"Yes papa, let's get back home. I can't wait to tell Daisy that I know how Winter must feel, because I now have a mamma too," said Emily.

Holly laughed and walked between the children, one arm around each of them. Frank helped her into the wagon. Jake climbed in and sat on her lap. Emily sat in the middle. Frank covered them all in the quilt and walked around and picked up the reins, clicked with his tongue and soon Buck and the wagon all got underway.

Holly was so saturated with the events of the day that she just sat back and relished in the peace and comfort of inclusion. She realized with a start that this was a feeling she would become accustomed to. But no matter how used to it she became, she would never cease being grateful. Quietly, she gave a prayer of thanks.

Once home there were chores to do, just as Frank had promised. The heaping measure of Holly's anticipation of Christmas morning had not even begun to meet the yield of blessings bestowed upon the family on Christmas day.

Frank brought in a plucked partridge that he had shot and cleaned earlier that morning. He helped Holly prepare and roast it in the oven. Emily peeled potatoes and carrots. Jake fed the pigs and freshened Daisy's stall. All the chores were done like clockwork, as though everyone had practiced their part to perfection. Before she knew it, they were all seated and Holly prepared to say grace. She drew her breath in, but Frank's voice spoke in her stead.

"Bless us all this Christmas day," he said. "We know that all blessings come from God above and we have been abundantly blessed. Thank the Lord that

Holly answered my letter and said yes. I think that was the Lord's doing. All our lives are better since she came to us. Thank you Lord for delivering Holly unto us. Holly loved the Lord so well that she brought all of us back to Him. It was her love that led me back to the Lord. It was her love that taught me I had been angry with the Lord. Forgive me for not wanting Christmas, not wanting anything to do with God. Holly saved us. She has made us once again a family. Thanks be to God. All blessings come from Thee."

Holly needed a moment before she could say anything. She swallowed hard and blinked. That was quite a speech Frank had made. "I didn't save all of you. You saved me," Holly replied.

"It was God's mercy that saved us all," Emily said quietly.

Holly marveled at the girl's wisdom. "Yes, Emily, I think that is what it was."

Holly looked around the table. Jake's face was bright and pink and full of good cheer as he took a bite of pheasant. Emily's face was glowing. Frank looked open and serene. His face was still strong and lean but it no longer looked carved out of wood. His eyes were alight with warmth. Their Christmas dinner was the sweetest, richest, most wonderful meal that she could ever remember.

There was roasted pheasant on the table with family all around, a marriage that was no longer something bargained for but something earned as well as freely given. For her part, it had required patience and bravery and, most importantly, a dependence upon faith. For Frank's part, it had demanded that he relinquish his anger towards God and open his heart to love another again.

Holly added something else to Frank's grace. *Dear Lord, thank you for granting my heart's desire: a family for Christmas.*

ABOUT THE AUTHOR

Faith Austen is a city gal turned cattle ranch wife, all in the name of love. She lives among green pastures with her darling hubby and three children where she'll be found either cooking up a storm in the kitchen or cuddled up with her Labrador Sam and a good book! She is devoted to her family and God and loves to write sweet, wholesome romance for like-minded women.

Made in the USA
Monee, IL
03 July 2021

72869140R00114